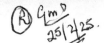

'So, Miss Henderson, beneath that marshmallow appearance of yours beats a heart of steel, does it?'

Poppy looked at him indignantly. 'Marshmallow? What's that supposed to mean?'

By now Fergus definitely looked as though he was enjoying himself. 'All that pale, fluffy hair—and all that muck you've got plastered around your eyes. And that sticky-looking stuff on your mouth—you look just like a sugar-coated piece of confectionery!'

There was a long pause.

Well. She could tell him what he could do with his typewriter and head for the door. Or could she? No other agency would touch her, with such little experience. And she *did* need the job.

Poppy dropped her handbag over the back of the nearest chair with a fluid movement. She needed the job, and he needed a secretary.

She gave him the benefit of a sweetly innocent smile. 'If I look like a sugar-coated piece of confectionery, Dr Browne, then your shirt looks like the crumpled-up bit of wrapper from it! And now, if we've finished our little chat, perhaps we could get on with some work?'

He opened his mouth, and shut it again. How wonderful to see him looking so nonplussed!

Sharon Wirdnam has been a waitress, a photographer and a cook. She then trained as a nurse and a medical secretary and found that she enjoyed working in a caring environment. She decided that one day she would write about romance against the dramatic backdrop of hospital life.

She was encouraged to write by her doctor husband after the birth of their two children, and much of her medical information comes from him, and from friends. She lives in Surrey, where her husband is a GP.

Previous Titles

A MEDICAL LIAISON
TO BREAK A DOCTOR'S HEART
NURSE IN THE OUTBACK

For Gerald and
Gill O'Rourke

SPECIALIST IN LOVE

BY
SHARON WIRDNAM

MILLS & BOON LIMITED
ETON HOUSE   18–24 PARADISE ROAD
RICHMOND   SURREY   TW9 1SR

First published in Great Britain 1991
by Mills & Boon Limited

© Sharon Wirdnam 1991

Australian copyright 1991

ISBN 0 263 12778 8

Set in 10½ on 12 pt Linotron Times
15-9103-47563
Typeset in Great Britain by Centracet, Cambridge
Made and printed in Great Britain

CHAPTER ONE

POPPY HENDERSON didn't look particularly Irish; in fact at that moment she looked more like a hurricane gone out of control, thought Ella as she watched her flatmate whirl into the sitting-room, brandishing a piece of paper and whooping with joy.

She didn't *sound* particularly Irish either; she just had an unusually soft voice which took on a gentle lilt if she was feeling tired or excited. Like now.

'Tra-la!' she sang. 'The quick brown fox jumps over the lazy dog!'

Ella glanced up again from her newspaper, only mildly perturbed—she was long used to Poppy's excessive enthusiasm.

'I beg your pardon?'

'The quick brown fox jumps over the lazy dog,' repeated Poppy, grinning happily.

'I should see your doctor about it if I were you,' suggested Ella. 'I always knew you were crazy—but now I've got proof!'

Poppy collapsed into an armchair, throwing her feet over the side. 'No, silly. That was my typing test—do you realise that that particular sentence uses every letter of the alphabet?'

'No, I didn't actually!'

'And this evening I got it word-perfect—over and

5

over again—at fifty words a minute. I'm Mrs Johnson's prize pupil and she's even trying to fix me up with a job!'

Ella sighed and put the newspaper down, abandoning all attempts to read it. When Poppy was in this kind of mood she wouldn't get a moment's peace. 'You're not really going through with all this, are you? Throwing up your job at Maxwells and everything?'

'It's done! The deed is done!' announced Poppy dramatically. 'I've left. Seriously,' she wrinkled her upturned nose, 'I'm sick of being a beautician. Trying to convince women who need to lose thirty pounds that new Blanko face cream will make them look like Kim Basinger! Having to lie through my teeth every time they ask me whether such-and-such eye-shadow enhances their eyes—when a blindfold is about the only thing that would!'

'Poppy!'

'At least when I'm a secretary I'll be doing something really *useful*.' Her eyes took on a dreamy, faraway expression. 'Who knows? I could end up as the indispensable right-hand woman of some archaeologist—searching for ancient tombs somewhere in Egypt. . .'

'Hasn't it already been done in a film with Harrison Ford?' interposed Ella drily. 'You're much more likely to end up typing invoices for some importer in a ghastly windowless office somewhere in the town.'

'Honestly, Ella,' Poppy reproached her, 'you're the world's biggest pessimist!'

'Realist, you mean.'

'Anyway,' she announced airily, 'we shall see. I register at Trumps Temporary Agency tomorrow. Mrs Johnson's friend runs it.'

'I hope you're going to tone your image down a bit first,' said Ella, in some alarm.

'Nonsense! They'll have to take me as I am.'

Which was why Mrs Johnson's old college friend, a Miss Webb, blinked slightly as Poppy breezed into Trumps Temporaries.

She *had*, in fact, toned her image down slightly, but Miss Webb wasn't to know that. She saw across her desk a very slender young woman, her endlessly long legs encased in tight black leggings and topped with a huge fluffy mohair sweater on which Winnie-the-Pooh was licking from a jar of hunny.

The pale blonde hair obviously owed little of its abundance of curls and startling shade to nature, and the large violet eyes were enhanced by a subtle shading of at least three different coloured eye-shadows. From her ears swung two enormous silver ear-rings, and Miss Webb privately wondered how she managed to walk on such high heels.

But within several minutes of talking to her Miss Webb knew that her old friend's lavish praise had not been unjustified. The girl was indeed talented— bright, witty and quite overwhelmingly honest, a point which Miss Webb commented on.

'That's one of the reasons why I want to leave,' explained Poppy earnestly, leaning over the desk to emphasise what she was saying, silver bangles clanking like a brass band. 'The whole business of being a beautician is one of deceit—people don't want the truth. They *want* to believe that their skin is as soft as a rose petal. It's one of the best kept secrets in the world that the only people lots of make-up looks good on are those who really don't need to wear any.'

Miss Webb thought Poppy herself was one of those people, but refrained from comment. Instead she started to explain the uncertain world of 'temping'.

'I haven't very much in at the moment, I'm afraid. The best I can offer you is going to be odd days here and there, which can be a little unsettling, but things should pick up soon.'

Poppy brightened a little on hearing this. 'Oh, well. Just so long as I can pay the rent!'

Miss Webb began sorting through a box of cards in front of her. 'Let's just see what we have here. . .' she began, when the telephone on her desk began to jangle noisily.

'Excuse me,' she murmured, and picked up the instrument. 'Hello? Trumps Temporaries. How may I help you?'

Poppy then heard an intriguing one-sided conversation, peppered with half a dozen 'oh, no's!' and several terse asides of 'that man!' When she eventually replaced the receiver, Miss Webb turned her eyes on Poppy.

'I think we may be able to help one another, my dear. I think I have just the job for you.'

'You do?' Poppy sat up in her chair.

'I do indeed, working for Dr Fergus Browne at Highchester Hospital.'

'But I'm not a medical secretary,' protested Poppy. 'I couldn't possibly work for a doctor.'

'You'll soon pick it up—a bright girl like you,' said Miss Webb soothingly. 'And besides, I have no one else to send—his latest girl has just walked out.' She saw Poppy raise her eyebrows enquiringly. 'I'm afraid I can't deny he's a difficult man, Miss Henderson. Very difficult. He's used about seven girls from my agency, and not one of them has agreed to stay. Quite the opposite, in fact—they seem to leave in a flurry of tears. He seems to have quite a ridiculous effect on them, though for myself, I fail to see why. I'm being frank with you, Miss Henderson, because I believe you're the kind of young lady who stands up for herself.' She gave a kind smile. 'And on no account are you to allow him to bully you.'

Poppy gulped. Did she have any choice? 'OK, Miss Webb. I'll do it. When do I start?'

Miss Webb gave another smile, more apologetic this time. 'In about ten minutes?'

The hospital was within walking distance of the agency, and it was the first time Poppy had ever been inside. She shivered a little. The long corridor seemed to be very dark and draughty. She felt as though she needed a dregree in map-reading to find Dr Browne's offices, and she was slightly taken aback by the information proffered by the jokey girl at the reception desk whom she had asked for directions.

'Working for the Professor, are you?' She pulled a face. 'Rather you than me!'

Poppy set off in search of the lift. A Professor! Miss Webb hadn't told her *that*. He must be really high-powered, and ancient, no doubt. What was he going to say when he discovered that the girl they had sent him had only recently passed her typing test after a year of going to evening classes?

The offices on the tenth floor of the building were like a labyrinth, and she got lost about four times, wandering around in circles through identical-looking corridors before eventually locating an undistinguished door which bore the legend 'F. Browne—Dermatology'. Poppy was surprised. For a Professor's it looked a very dismal kind of office. Why, when she had worked at Maxwells, even the catering supervisor had resided in a far grander-looking room than this one!

She knocked on the door and waited, but no one replied. She tried again, but there was still no answer. Well, there was no doubt that Professor Browne was expecting her. She turned the handle and walked in.

It was not as she expected—inside there was total chaos, with books absolutely everywhere. Poppy had never seen so many books. They stood in high piles on almost every inch of the floor, so that she had to pick her way over them gingerly. They almost obscured every bit of the surface of the enormous mahogany desk that stood at the far corner of the room. And there was still no sign of her new boss.

At that moment the door flew open, and Poppy turned round to confront a very tall, lean man who was staring at her as if he'd just seen an apparition.

Light grey eyes came to rest first on her ear-rings, and then, with open astonishment, on the high black patent shoes she wore.

'Good grief,' he said faintly. 'Don't tell me you actually walked here in those things?'

She didn't know who he was, but judging from the extremely crumpled shirt he wore and the faded cords she guessed he was one of the maintenance men. And one who needed putting in his place too—he needn't think he could be so rude to the Professor's new secretary!

'How do you think I got here?' she demanded. 'Flew?'

'I should think that if you shook your head violently enough, the centrifugal force generated by the momentum of those ridiculous ear-rings would be enough to propel you into the outer stratosphere!' he returned.

She could see that sarcasm was going to be wasted on him. And on second thoughts, he didn't sound a bit like a maintenance man—why, the sentence he had just snapped back at her sounded as if you would need an 'A' level in physics just to understand it! Surely he couldn't be. . .?

No. She quashed the idea firmly. Well-spoken he might be, but a doctor he most definitely wasn't. Doctors wore suits, and looked responsible. Staid and trustworthy—like dear old Dr Evans at home. They certainly didn't tower at over six feet, lean and fit, making them look as if they'd be more suited to skiing down the side of some mountain. And quite apart from the crumpled shirt and the too-casual cords, no doctor on earth would be seen wearing a pink tie with *purple spots* all over it!

She decided to try a different tack. 'Can I help you?' she asked him, rather primly.

His mouth, which she automatically noted was quite a nice shape, set itself into a thin, uncompromising line. The light grey eyes allowed themselves a humourless glint.

'I doubt it,' he returned, continuing to stare at her with a kind of fascinated horror.

Time, without doubt, to let Mr High and Mighty know exactly to whom he was speaking. Poppy set her own glossy mouth into a line which unconsciously imitated his own.

'Do you realise to whom you're speaking?' she enquired archly, anticipating his discomfiture with glee, when his lazy reply completely threw her.

'Certainly. The latest in a long line of extremely unsatisfactory temporary secretaries which have been dredged up by your agency, I imagine.' He raised his very dark eyebrows and smiled. 'Am I correct?'

Poppy had rarely in her life been speechless, but she was now. Surely he couldn't be. . .?

'But you don't look a bit like a Professor!' she protested, her long, pink-painted nails gripping on to the table for support.

The dark brows grew together in a frown, and the grey eyes glared. 'I beg your pardon?' he asked coldly.

Poppy laughed nervously. 'You! You aren't what

I expected! When they said I'd be working for the Professor, I imagined someone much older.'

What *had* she said to offend him? The grey eyes were sending out sparks which could have ignited the desk.

'Are you trying to be funny?' he demanded.

'How so?' She was genuinely bewildered and she knew that her reply was casual and ungrammatical, but she was still trying to forget that this brute of a man wasn't someone who had come to tamper with the central heating.

'Who told you I was a Professor?' he snapped.

For a moment Poppy wished she was back at Maxwells, handing out sapphire eye-shadow to corpulent women of sixty who should have known better. She tried a smile which used to melt the general floor manager's heart.

'The girl on the reception desk,' she explained. 'I asked her where I could find Dr Browne and she said "working for the Professor, are you?"' Poppy's lips clamped hastily shut, as she recalled the next comment, which had been 'rather you than me!' She began to get a good idea what the receptionist had meant! 'Have I said something wrong?' she asked, fixing her huge violet eyes on his face.

'It's a joke,' he told her flatly.

'Well, you're hardly doubled up laughing yourself,' she quipped, and was rewarded with a look which could have rivalled Medusa's.

'A poor joke.' He pulled one of the textbooks on the desk towards him, glancing down at the open page before returning his gaze to her. 'It dates from my days as a student—Miss——?'

'Henderson,' said Poppy helpfully. 'But you can call me Poppy.'

'Miss Henderson,' he continued, ignoring her friendly overture. 'Do you have much experience of hospitals, Miss Henderson?'

'None, I'm afraid,' she said brightly.

'I thought not.' He gave a weary sigh. 'Then allow me to enlighten you about some fairly typical behaviour. If, as a student, you tend to commit that awful sin of enjoying your work, and pursuing it with any degree of vigour, then you're labelled a bore. Or a swot. I was known as the "Professor".'

Poppy's heart sank. Trust her to have revived some ancient and hated nickname!

'If, on the other hand, you do as little work as possible, date every woman in your year, and are never to be seen without a glass of beer in your hand, you'll win the admiration of your peers and be labelled a jolly good chap!' The rather nicely shaped mouth twisted again, and Poppy tried, and failed, to imagine him in this second role.

Oh, well. It had been a good try, but poor old Miss Webb was going to have yet another temp leave—and this one was probably going to break the record for having been there the shortest time.

Grumpy seemed to have forgotten she was there—his attention had switched suddenly from moaning at her to scanning a page of the textbook he'd just moved, and muttering 'mmm' just as if he'd bitten into an unexpectedly delicious cake.

Poppy began to hitch her bag over her shoulder, uncertain of how best to get out of there.

She cleared her throat, but he didn't even look up. She coughed quietly, but still he took no notice, just carried on reading. The sooner she was out of there the better—the man was a lunatic!

'Er—I suppose I'd better be going, Dr Browne.'

He looked at her then, and she got a good idea of how some poor unsuspecting mouse must feel before the cat pounces on it.

'What?' he demanded.

'I said I'd better be going now. I'm sorry if I appeared rude. . .'

'Going?' He slung the book down, and Poppy blinked with surprise to see 'Fergus C. Browne' on the front of it. 'And just where do you think you're going, Miss Henderson?'

'Well, you won't want me now, will you?' she asked bluntly. 'Not now that I've reminded you of what a rotten time you had as a student.'

And suddenly he laughed, showing superb white teeth. The relaxed movement affected his whole stance, so that for the briefest second he looked so—so gorgeous, there was no other way to describe it, that her heart did a funny little dance all on its own. There was even a twinkle in the forbidding eyes.

'On the contrary, Miss Henderson,' he drawled, 'I had a very happy time as a student. Very happy indeed.'

And, witnessing this astonishing transformation, she could well believe it.

'As for my "wanting" you,' the smile had switched off more quickly than the Christmas tree lights on Twelfth Night, 'what I want, and what I've been wanting for over fourteen months now, is a secretary who can type without making a mistake every other word. Someone who can be pleasant on the telephone, and helpful. Someone who will listen to what's being asked of her. Someone who will not terrify or intimidate my patients. Someone who will not sniff, or sulk, or file her nails and look bored. Someone who will not attempt to engage me in what I believe is popularly known as "chit-chat".

'I don't care what you've watched on television. I am not interested in soap operas, or the Royal Family. I want someone with more than two neurones to rub together.' He watched her questioningly. 'Do you think that what I'm asking is unreasonable, Miss Henderson?'

Poppy could hardly believe what she was hearing. What an insufferable pig! She remembered Miss Webb's parting words, that on no account was she to let him bully her. Damn right, she wouldn't!

She glowered at him. 'Yes, I do! And more than that—it's the most patronising thing I've ever heard!'

The watchful eyes grew thoughtful. 'You think I'm exaggerating the tendencies of your predecessors?'

He was regarding her with interest, as though he actually cared about what she might think, and she felt her cheeks grow a little hot, irritatingly flustered by this quirky individual.

'They probably did do some of those things—if not all of them. But perhaps they filed their nails because they *were* bored. Have you asked yourself whether you gave them enough work to do? Maybe they tried to chat to you because you were so prickly and they were trying to cheer you up. Their bad telephone manner could have just been insecurity. They probably hated being here as much as you hated having them here.'

He had shoved a whole pile of books aside and had perched on the edge of the desk, his long cord-clad legs spread in front of him. Poppy had to concentrate very hard not to stare at his awful tie.

'Do go on,' he murmured. 'This is fascinating.'

She glanced at him suspiciously. Was he being sarcastic? But what the hell? She'd finish what she was going to say now.

'You obviously don't like having a secretary,' she offered, 'being reliant on someone else—and so you treat them badly; and everyone knows that if you treat people badly then they behave badly!'

The eyebrows retreated still further into a lock of the light brown hair. 'Do they, indeed?'

She couldn't believe he could be so stupid! 'Of course they do!' she declared. 'If you kick a dog, then the dog becomes bad-tempered and aggressive and neurotic. If you mistreat a child it won't develop normally, and pu-punitive punishments handed out to juvenile delinquents are far more likely to have a bad effect—than involvement and hard work.'

'Punitive, hm? That's a good word, Miss Henderson,' he remarked.

'I read it in a newspaper last week,' she told him proudly, before returning his gaze mulishly. Was he making fun of her?

The long legs had shifted slightly. 'I trust that you're not comparing yourself to a dog, or a child, or a juvenile delinquent? How old are you, by the way?'

She really couldn't see the point of prolonging this interview. 'Twenty.'

A brief smile. He should do that more often, she thought.

'Well, you nearly qualified, didn't you?' he remarked.

'What for?'

'The juvenile part, naturally,' and he began to laugh.

'Very funny!' The surprising thing was that she didn't feel any awe about talking to him so frankly. She still couldn't believe that he was really a doctor, to her he seemed more like some overgrown school-boy, and one who had had his own way for far too long.

'How old are you?' she asked.

'How old do you think I am?'

Poppy sighed. 'If you knew how many times I'd heard that! I'd say you were about thirty.'

'Excellent! You're a year out—I'm thirty-one.'

'I'm good on ages,' she said smugly, remembering the countless times that crêpe-lined faces had been thrust over the counter towards her at Maxwells with a plea for a foundation to hide the blemishes, usually accompanied by the lie that 'I'm only just forty'.

She blinked after her little reverie to find him tapping one long finger on the side of the desk. He wore no gold band and she found herself wondering whether or not he was married. Pity the poor woman who found herself saddled with Dr Browne!

'So, Miss Henderson, beneath that marshamallow appearance of yours beats a heart of steel, does it?'

She looked at him indignantly. 'Marshmallow? What's that supposed to mean?'

By now he definitely looked as though he was enjoying himself. 'All that pale, fluffy hair—and all that muck you've got plastered around your eyes. And that sticky-looking stuff on your mouth—you look just like a sugar-coated piece of confectionery!'

There was a long pause.

Well. She could tell him what he could do with his typewriter and head for the door. Or could she? Hadn't Miss Webb told her that this was the only job she had? And Miss Webb was a good friend of her tutor; she had gone to her highly recommended. No other agency would touch her, with such little experience. And she *did* need the job. She had left Maxwells now, and it might have been boring but at least it had paid very well. How else was she going to find the rent?

She dropped her handbag over the back of the nearest chair with a fluid movement. She needed the job, and he needed a secretary. She would work for the obnoxious man, but she was going to take Miss Webb's advice literally—and damn the consequences!

She gave him the benefit of a sweetly innocent

smile. 'If I look like a sugar-coated piece of confectionery, Dr Browne, then your shirt looks like the crumpled-up bit of wrapper from it! And now, if we've finished our little chat, perhaps we could get on with some work?'

He opened his mouth, and shut it again. How wonderful to see him looking so nonplussed!

'You'll have to do it without me,' he said carelessly. 'I'm off to a meeting now. Perhaps you'd like to tidy up a bit?'

The way he said it suggested that she was little more than a skivvy, and Poppy gritted her teeth, but said nothing.

'I'll be in early Monday morning, so I'll show you the ropes then. That is, if you're coming back on Monday?'

Put like that, it sounded like a challenge. There was nothing more she would have liked than to have told him she was never going to set foot in his dark, untidy mausoleum of an office again, but she was not going to give him that pleasure. That was what was known as cutting off your nose to spite your face.

'Oh, don't worry about that, Dr Browne,' she told him. 'I'll be back.'

She bent over her handbag as if she'd found something tremendously important in it, and didn't look at him once as he strode out of the room.

CHAPTER TWO

AFTER he had disappeared, Poppy heaved a huge sigh of relief and sat back in one of the chairs to survey the contents of his office more closely. Thank heavens she had worn her leggings! There was dust everywhere—generated, no doubt, by the heaps of books. She picked up the book he had been reading and regarded it with interest. It was entitled *Diagnostic Dermatology* and was indeed written by the man for whom she now worked.

The book was new, the dust cover shiny, and the whole volume had that delicious smell which all new books have. Poppy loved books. She lived for them. And books had taught her almost everything she knew. When you'd missed chunks of your education because teachers would never stay in the remote part of the country you'd grown up in, you quickly realised that there was a lot of catching up to do!

On the inside of the dust cover there was a short piece about the author. It told her that Fergus C. Browne—she wondered idly what the 'C' stood for—had been educated at Cambridge and then at King's College Hospital. That, as well as being one of the youngest consultant dermatologists in the country, he had also written papers on infectious diseases, and the psychological effects of having a chronic skin condition diagnosed.

21

Poppy frowned. It was a pity he didn't apply some psychological reasoning to the way he treated his staff—or, better still, use a bit of common sense. What was it going to be like working for such a capricious individual? Were they going to be engaged in running verbal battles all day long? Would he continue to be so incredibly rude about the way she looked?

She gave a long sigh. Better stop being so pensive and get on with the job. She wouldn't put it past him to come breezing back in here after an hour, just to check what she had accomplished in his absence!

But how to go about tidying up his disgusting den? She didn't want him accusing her of misplacing all his books, but clearly she couldn't set up an efficient workplace if she had to keep stepping over haphazardly sited piles.

In the centre of the room was an enormous, old-fashioned fireplace, with a large recess on either side. The two spaces were just crying out for bookshelves. She scrabbled around on his desk and eventually found an unused notepad and Biro, and began to make a list.

In her rather rounded script, she wrote:

1. Have bookshelves erected ASAP!!!
2. Phone library re. most effective way of classifying books.
3. Buy a plant!

The hospital telephonist gave her the number of the maintenance department, and Poppy had to bite back a giggle when she remembered how she'd mistaken the illustrious Dr Browne for one of them. Thank goodness she hadn't blurted that out!

A bored voice answered the phone and informed her that there was no one in the department who could help at that time, but if she left her number then they would get back to her later that afternoon, and with that Poppy had to be content.

Next she rang the local library and spoke to a very helpful girl there who explained that, as most large libraries were computerised, their systems would be inappropriate for a small, private collection of books. She suggested that alphabetical filing by author would be best, with a cross-reference file for subject matter. She also advised a marker system, in case any of the books were lent out.

While she waited for the maintenance department to ring her back, Poppy sorted all the books out into alphabetical order and placed them in neat groups around the room. It took her over an hour to do this, and by the end of it her mouth felt dry and her clothes were covered in a fine layer of dust. She had long since removed her mohair sweater, and her pink T-shirt proved plenty warm enough. She brushed her hands down the side of her leggings and glanced around. Some order had been restored, at least. She hunted around for something to drink, but found nothing, and since she didn't want to risk missing the telephone call regarding the bookshelves she did without, but added, 'Buy a kettle!' to her list.

At five minutes to five they rang back and she explained her predicament, but not even all her charm could sway the dour-sounding man at the other end, who seemed the worst kind of petty bureaucrat, and obviously relished refusing her request.

'If we put shelves up for you, then everyone would want them,' he droned.

'But we're not everyone!' wailed Poppy. 'And if you don't tell anyone, we won't.'

He was now not only impervious to pleading, he was disapproving.

'We have to work within the system, miss,' he said sternly. 'And as for not letting anyone know—I have to complete my work sheets in triplicate, so everyone would know.'

'Oh, for goodness' sake!' said Poppy crossly. 'I've never heard anything so ridiculous in my life! Talk about a spirit of co-operation! Thanks for nothing!'

She put the phone down. Now what was she going to do? She had almost barricaded her desk in with the wretched things, and she could just see Dr Fergus Browne storming in tomorrow and accusing her of mucking around with his precious books—he was just the kind of contrary person to do that!

But wait a minute—he wasn't going to be in tomorrow, and neither, officially, was she. Tomorrow was Saturday and the day after was Sunday. Which gave her two clear days to get the shelves up!

She gave a small smile as she mentally applauded her brilliant brainwave, and at five-thirty she set off home, to tell Ella all about what had happened.

* * *

Ella slammed her way into the flat at just gone seven to find it strangely silent. Poppy usually had music blaring out from the sitting-room.

'Poppy?' she called hesitantly.

'In here! I'm in the bathroom.'

Ella hung up her jacket and left her basket on the table and, picking up an apple which she began crunching into, walked into the bathroom, where she found Poppy, clad only in a black lace bra and knickers, bending down and peering at herself in the badly placed mirror.

Without turning round she spoke in a gloomy voice.

'Do I remind you of a marshmallow?'

Ella swallowed a pip by mistake. '*What*? I knew this would happen. I always said it—one day Poppy Henderson will finally flip!'

'Shut up—I'm serious. Do I or do I not remind you of a marshmallow?'

'Of course you don't. You remind me of Marilyn Monroe—everyone says so.'

'Marilyn Monroe was fat.'

'She wasn't fat, she was curvaceous. Nice bust, small waist, good legs—just like you.'

'Fat,' muttered Poppy dejectedly. 'Do you think I wear too much make-up?'

Ella shifted uncomfortably. 'It is a bit much, sometimes—especially by day.' She saw Poppy's face and hurriedly changed her tack. 'I mean, it was different when you were working at Maxwells—that whole look was part of your job. But you've got such lovely skin and eyes that it seems rather a shame to cover them up. And if I had hair as shiny as yours I certainly wouldn't dye it blonde.'

'You would if it was mousy,' Poppy pointed out, the harsh light falling on her finely-boned face to cast deep shadows under her cheekbones.

'It's golden-brown, not mousy—and what the hell has got into you tonight, Poppy? I've never known you to be so negative. Do I take it that you're one of the many unemployed, and that this is responsible for a face as long as your arm?'

Poppy shook her head, so that the pale curls flew like angry snakes around her face.

'Not at all—I've got a job, and that's the problem.'

Ella's face broke into a huge grin. 'What are you talking about? You've got a job, that's fabulous! You should be jumping up and down for joy and offering me a large glass of wine to celebrate.'

Poppy sighed. 'Wait till you hear! I've got a job working for the most bad-tempered doctor you could ever imagine.'

'A doctor? But you can't. . . I mean, you don't. . .'

'Exactly,' agreed Poppy grimly. 'I know nothing about medicine. I don't understand what he does, and I certainly haven't got a clue how to spell the words.'

'Then how come. . .?'

'I'm the agency's last hope. He's driven away countless others. And that's the second bad thing— he hates secretaries. From what he's said I can imagine that a slug eating his prize cabbage would get more respect and affection!'

'He sounds ghastly.'

'Believe me, he is. Then there's the third awful thing,' added Poppy.

'Go on.'

'Someone jokingly told me that he was a professor, and so that's what I called him—after, I might add, I mistook him for one of the maintenance men.'

Ella stifled a giggle. 'Oh, Poppy!'

'How was I to know that "Professor" was the nickname he hated which he's had since medical school?'

'You're making all this up!'

'Oh, that I were! And now I've got to try and get some shelves up in his room before Monday, or else he'll hit the roof when he sees how I've rearranged his blessed books. Do you have Mick Douglas's number?'

'It's in the book,' replied her friend with a fond but sinking heart. Why had Poppy insisted on rocking the boat in order to do a job that she clearly wasn't suited for?

Professor indeed! She couldn't see this job last the week out.

Fergus left the side room and walked quickly into the office, his professional demeanour of calm assurance crumpling into brief despair. It never got any easier. How could it?

The charge nurse looked over at him sympathetically. 'Coffee?' he asked.

Fergus shook his head. 'No, thanks, Geoff.' He began to write in the patient's notes 'systemic lumpus erythematosus'. In his untidy hand he scrawled the inevitable syptoms—the outaneous signs which included the well-known 'butterfly' ery-thema on the face, frontal alopecia, mucosal ulcer-ation. He refrained from writing the two words which the disorder signified to most of the staff on the ward—potentially fatal.

Today was Sunday and he shouldn't even have been here, but how could he not be here? He had come in himself as if to lessen the blow of the news he'd had to impart.

But how did you tell a young girl of twenty-three, poised on the brink of her professional and emotional life, that she might not see the year out? A beautiful young girl with the face of a Madonna, a classical pianist with so much life and talent in those hands, whose equally young husband had stared at him with bewildered eyes, as if he were some idiot who had made some fundamental and terribly wrong mistake, not the consultant in charge of his wife's case.

He finished writing in the notes and stood up slowly.

'What are you up to today, Fergus?' asked Geoff. 'Nice day for a country pub!'

Fergus half smiled. 'No such luck, I'm afraid— I've an article waiting at home which won't write itself.'

Geoff groaned. 'Rather you than me!'

Fergus left the ward, mentally agreeing with the

charge-nurse. He wished he *had* arranged something today, something which was a million miles away from this damned job.

Still, he'd feel good once it was written, and afterwards he'd reward himself with the luxury of all the Sunday papers and a plate of *spaghetti alla carbonara* while Vivaldi played gently in the background. An almost perfect evening.

He was just about to leave by the main entrance when he remembered the book. Blast it! His run-in with the latest dizzy blonde secretary meant that he had left the office on Friday without Jacob's definitive work on skin diseases, without which he couldn't hope to write the kind of well-founded article the *Journal* would naturally expect from him. Thank goodness he'd remembered before he'd gone all the way home.

He was pleased to be able to arrive at the door to his office without encountering anyone he knew. He had been dreading running into Veronica Entwistle—the staff nurse on one of his wards, who had told him at least four times that she was on an early Saturday, followed by a late on Sunday, 'so if you're short of company, Fergus. . .' The woman was about as subtle as a sergeant-major!

As he turned the handle of the door he became aware of two discrepancies—a muffled expletive assailed his ears and he heard some tinny kind of banal rubbish playing, which he assumed was the radio.

He flung the door open and the first thing he saw was the sight of a very long, very slender leg, clad in faded denim so clinging that he was immediately convinced that the wearer's circulation would be seriously affected. The shapely thigh became an extremely attractive bottom and in turn a tiny waist topped by the most splendid bust he'd ever seen.

Fergus had been many things in his life, but he had never before been quite so taken aback, and it took a few seconds for it to dawn on him that he was standing staring like an idiot at the curvaceous shape of his new secretary. She was standing frozen into immobility, screwdriver in her hand. In the corner stood a worried-looking fair-haired young man whose huge shoulders and stature marked him out as a born rugby player.

Fergus set his mouth in a grim line. 'Perhaps you'd care to explain what you're doing hanging off a step-ladder, Miss Henderson? No, don't tell me, let me guess! Your local amateur dramatic society is holding auditions for its production of *Peter Pan*, and you're just getting in a bit of practice?'

Sarcastic so-and-so! thought Poppy as she carefully picked her way down to his level, peering up at him with a fixed smile on her face.

'I'm putting up some bookshelves for you, Dr Browne,' she informed him brightly. 'Do you like them?'

It was true. He could see symmetrical shelves, four rows of them already in place on one side of the fireplace, and at the same moment he realised that she'd changed his whole office round.

'What?' he boomed, so loudly that Poppy took a step back. 'What have you done with my *books*?'

Poppy smiled as patiently as if she were dealing with a simpleton. 'I've been sorting them out for you, Dr Browne. Obviously we couldn't have them lying around in piles on the floor, could we?'

'Oh, couldn't we?' he snapped petulantly. 'Well, I want a copy of. . .' He rattled the name of the textbook off quicker than a laser. 'And I don't want it next week—I want it *now*. So either you produce the book within the two minutes I'm giving you, or you find yourself back in the dole queue first thing in the morning!'

Damn cheek, thought Poppy rebelliously as she scurried over to the alcove—she'd never been in a dole queue in her life.

The silence in the office was like a time-bomb waiting to go off. Fergus stood looking out of the window, his back to the giant in the corner, studiously avoiding all contact with him.

Mick Douglas watched as Poppy scrabbled to find the list she'd made of all the volumes. To think he could have been down the pub with his mates, instead of stuck in this chilly room with this hot-headed maniac! The guy needed locking up. Fancy speaking to her like that! Mick sighed. Poppy had a lot to answer for. She had a way of looking at you that made it impossible to refuse her anything, and she had meant it when she'd said that *she* wanted to put the shelves up, not him. 'You're just here in an advisory capacity,' she had told him grandly. Mick eyed the brooding figure by the window warily. He must be a good twenty pounds lighter, but he'd hate to get on the bad side of *him*.

Fergus had begun drumming his fingers on the windowsill as the final seconds ticked away, when Poppy gave a great shout of delight.

'Here we are! *Dermatological Disorders Discovered* by Professor Donald Jacob.' She held the book out with smiling eyes, the laughter quickly leaving them when she saw the expression on her boss's face as he strode over from the window to take the book from her.

'I wonder if you'd be good enough to step outside for a moment?' he asked in a deliberately polite voice which did nothing to disguise his ill-humour.

'Certainly, Dr Browne. I shan't be more than a moment, Mick,' she called to her friend. I hope. She had been reading *1984* by George Orwell last night, the bit where they had recited the old nursery rhyme: 'Here comes a candle to light you to bed. Here comes a chopper to chop off your head'. How appropriate that seemed just at this moment, following old Grumpy out into the corridor. 'Chip-chop. Chip-chop. The last man's. . .'

'Miss Henderson?'

'Dead!' she blurted out, before she could stop herself.

He frowned. 'I *beg* your pardon?'

She realised what she'd said. 'I'm so sorry, Dr Browne—I was miles away.'

'Obviously.'

He looked as if he'd spent the morning sucking a lemon—he was so sour-faced, she thought as she waited. He was bound to get rid of her now.

He was about to tell her not to bother coming in

tomorrow when he caught a glimpse of such a resigned expression on the naïve young face that he felt strangely touched. If you took away all the face paint and the fashionable clothes, underneath wasn't she a girl like any other, trying her best to survive in an increasingly hostile world?

And hadn't he rather admired the spunky way she had spoken to him on Friday? It was a sad but inevitable fact that the higher up your particular ladder you got, the more distance it created between you and the people around you. He disliked people toadying to him—simpering sycophants who thought that tacking 'yes, sir' on to the end of every sentence would make them an instant crony.

Apart from Catherine, he couldn't remember anyone who had spoken to him as directly as this girl in a long time.

He forced himself to be pleasant. 'It was good of you to give up your weekend to rearrange my office, but I would have preferred it if you'd consulted me first. . .'

'I will in future,' Poppy butted in eagerly.

Fergus sighed. She was like an exuberant young puppy, completely unsquashable. He rearranged the softer expression which had crept over his features and looked down at her sternly.

'In future, however, you will *not* bring your boy-friend into my office, not without my permission.'

'But he's not my. . .' she protested, but he shook his head.

'I'm not interested in your private life, as I hope you'll be uninterested in mine. And, now if you'll excuse me, I have an article to write. I'll see you first thing tomorrow morning.'

Weakly she nodded, leaning against the wall of the corridor as she watched him walk away, unsure whether to cheer or howl.

CHAPTER THREE

Poppy arrived punctually at her typewriter at nine
o'clock on Monday morning to find the office empty,
and she stood in the centre of the room rather
uncertainly, unsure of what to do next—she didn't
dare try to alter anything else, not without the
permission of Grumpy! And she had decided not to
introduce the kettle or any plants until she had a
better idea of just how long she would be staying!

One thing was for sure—his office looked a million times better—more spacious and less cluttered.
And what was it they said? A tidy room means a
tidy mind—maybe the quality of his articles would
improve, and then he'd be forever in her debt!

She was bent over her desk, flicking dust off the
electric typewriter and ineffectually moving pieces
of paper around for something to do, when the door
flew open with a crash and she looked up, startled,
expecting to see Dr Browne; instead she was con-
fronted by the sight of a girl of about sixteen, her
eyes red from crying, her hair flying wildly around
her face, and some poorly applied foundation
attempting to cover what Poppy could see were
angry red spots on her face.

'Where is he?' the girl demanded, on a note that
sounded as though it could become a sob without
very much provocation.

35

Poppy smiled encouragingly. 'You mean Dr Browne? I'm expecting him in any time now. Won't you take a seat?'

The girl flopped into the chair Poppy had indicated, and with trembling hands started fumbling around in her handbag. She pulled out a crumpled packet of cigarettes and had extracted and lit one, exhaling deeply, before Poppy could stop her. The familiar acrid smell of the smoke assailed Poppy's nostrils and she was filled with a wave of nausea.

She spoke as politely as possible. 'This is a hospital, you know. I don't think it's a very good idea if you smoke, do you?'

The girl stared at her belligerently. 'I don't think a lot of things are a good idea—like the fact that I resemble Frankenstein's monster with this face of mine, but there's not a lot I can do about it.' She took another deep drag of the cigarette.

Poppy coughed. The room was filling up with smoke and she couldn't bear it, and neither, she was pretty sure, would Dr Browne.

'Please put it out,' she requested firmly.

The girl's bottom lip jutted out. 'Why should I?'

'Because my uncle died of lung cancer through smoking, and I'd hate to think that you might do the same.' Her voice shook a little as she said it.

The girl looked up at her, distraught, her eyes filling with tears, and she held the cigarette out helplessly towards Poppy, bursting into noisy, child-like sobs.

Poppy took the cigarette and swiftly ran it under the tap of the sink in the corner, before dropping it in the waste-paper bin. She pulled out a paper handkerchief from her handbag and handed it to the crying girl.

'I'm so sorry,' the girl sobbed. 'I'm a horrible person. But it's not how he said it would be—he's got no *idea*!'

Poppy tried without success to make some kind of sense of the garbled sentence. 'Who?' she asked.

'Fergus,' sobbed the girl again. 'He doesn't know what it's really like.'

Fergus! It seemed strange for this wild young thing with the hurt young face to be on first-name terms with old Grumpy. Poppy wished she had had the courage of her convictions and had brought the wretched kettle in—at least then she could have made this poor child a cup of strong, sweet tea. Instead she handed her another hanky and smiled softly.

'Doesn't know what what's really like?' she probed gently.

'College!' The word came out in a sniffly sob.

'You mean you've just started college?' Poppy guessed.

'Yes. We thought it would be good if I did my "A" levels there—people would be more mature than they were at school. Some hopes! I've had to put up with cruel teasing for years at school, and we thought it would be different at college—but it isn't.'

By now Poppy was utterly confused. 'Teasing about what?'

The girl stared at her with a hard, cold face. 'This!' She pointed to the livid spots on her face.

'It's called acne—don't tell me you didn't notice?' she asked disbelievingly.

'I did notice, yes,' replied Poppy truthfully. 'But it wasn't the first thing I noticed—the first thing I noticed was how sad you looked.'

'If people flinched every time you came near them, you'd look sad,' the girl retaliated. 'If boys didn't want to kiss you, for fear of what they'd "catch"—you'd look sad too.' A bitter look crossed her face. 'Oh, what's the point? You'd never understand in a million years—no one can help, not even Fergus, unless he's got a magic wand which could give me a new skin.' She got up from the chair, dejection written in the slump of her shoulders. 'Tell him I called, won't you?' She started for the door.

Poppy rose to her feet, feeling utterly helpless. 'I don't even know your name?' she queried.

'It's Virginia—Virginia Barker.'

'Do stay and see him, Virginia,' Poppy pleaded. 'Now that you've come all this way, and you're upset—stay here and let me get you some coffee.'

But it was no use, Virginia had lifted her chin and was gone. Poppy sat in impotent silence. There had been such raw anger in the girl. Surely something could be done to help her?

The door opened again and there stood Dr Browne, a briefcase under one arm and a stack of papers under the other. He nodded at her, without the welcoming smile she would have wished for.

'All right?' he asked tersely.

Poppy arranged three pens in a straight line and looked up.

'Actually, no,' she told him calmly. 'A patient of yours has just been in here, sobbing and in a terrible state. A girl called Virginia Barker, saying that things are no better at college, that she's being teased there too.'

He put the papers on to his desk. 'Ah, yes—young Ginny. Why wouldn't she wait?'

'Because she was so upset, I told you. She said that no one could help her—she seemed rather desperate.'

He was removing his tweed jacket and hanging it over the back of his chair, to reveal a mauve and yellow plaid tie. 'I'll give her a call later,' he said, and with this he began pulling more papers out of his briefcase.

Poppy sat there, aghast. 'Is that all?' she demanded.

He looked up, gazing round the room, as if unsure whether the question had been directed at him. 'What?' he demanded.

She was undeterred by the angry note in his voice. 'I said is that all you're going to say? The girl was really *upset*, surely there must be something more that we can do than just give her a call later. You. . .'

'No—*you*! Listen to me for a minute, before you come out with any more of your naïve little clichés. Do you imagine for one moment that you're the only person who cares about her? Do you think I hold some instant cure here in my hands, which through some sadistic urge I'm refusing to give her? Well? Do you?'

Poppy's lips snapped shut. 'I was only trying. . .'

'Trying nothing! You were preaching to me. Of course she was upset. She's had acne since the age of fourteen—a time when most girls of that age are just beginning to adjust to their burgeoning sexuality. Ginny at that age would rather have had a cave to cower in than a discotheque to go to dance and flaunt her beauty and her youth. She's come a long way since then—despite the fact that with each year the acne has become progressively worse, culminating this year with a student teacher, albeit an ignorant one, asking Ginny to provide her with a doctor's certificate stating that the rash wasn't infectious. She even hinted delicately about AIDS. . .'

'But that's terrible!' Poppy gasped.

'Yes,' he agreed grimly, 'that's terrible, but that, I'm afraid, is life. It was then that Ginny decided that she must go to college, and I agreed with her, but tempered with my agreement was the warning that it wasn't all going to be plain sailing, that one of the most intrenchable characteristics of the human race is prejudice.

'So you see, my dear Miss Henderson, it comes as no surprise to me to learn that she's encountered it yet again, and I'd like to hear just what you suggest I do. Go down there and personally threaten to beat up anyone who's insulted her? Or do you think I should be down in the bowels of this building, inventing a new face for her?'

The depth of his anger was shattering, and Poppy felt close to tears, but she had the sense within herself to realise that the anger was not directed at her personally, that he was as upset by Ginny's problems as she was. But there was no doubt about one thing. That she owed him an apology.

'I'm very sorry, Dr Browne,' she said clearly. 'I spoke out of turn. I didn't know enough about her case, and I can assure you that it won't happen again.'

He rubbed at the soft brown hair on his temple, slightly mollified. 'Humph,' he muttered. 'At least you haven't stormed out, leaving me in the lurch. I made my point, but perhaps I didn't do it in the most tactful way—I do have the tendency to fly off the handle when I'm roused.'

Never! she thought, as her customary good humour returned. But she had an idea. 'Can I ask you something else, please, Dr Browne?'

'Not time off already?' he asked suspiciously.

What kind of women had he had working for him before? she wondered.

'No, nothing like that. It's just that I know some-one who deals with the importation of cosmetics. They bring in a lot of stuff from the States—there are new products on the market all the time. I just wondered whether I should speak to her, to ask if there's anything revolutionary in the line of conceal-ment products—I do know they exist.'

He looked unimpressed. 'Oh, they exist all right, and they're very useful for disguising birthmarks—port-wine stains and the like, but I've not heard of anything that's particularly efficacious for acne. Ginny's will probably have disappeared by the time she's twenty-five.'

But that's nearly ten years away, Poppy wanted to blurt out, but stopped herself in time.

'However, there's nothing to stop you trying,' he finished, and she flashed him a huge smile of gratitude.

'One thing, though,' he warned. 'Don't become too attached to her.'

'Why ever not?' she asked in surprise.

'Because she's vulnerable, because she'll probably like you—she's not past the age where she might hero-worship you. So you'll form an attachment with Ginny, she'll put her trust in you—and then you'll get bored with the job, and you'll be off.'

She wished he didn't have such a jaundiced view of everyone. His voice when he spoke was alive with passion and conviction; rarely had she met someone so quixotic, and she knew with some kind of uncanny conviction that she would not get bored with this job, with working for this man. She wanted this strange, prickly, grumpy individual to respect her— more than that, she wanted him to actually *like* her—but she suspected that winning his affection and respect wasn't going to be easy.

'I can't imagine the job boring me, Dr Browne,' she told him calmly. 'And I have no intention of leaving. What do you think of your bookshelves?'

He glanced at them critically. 'They're not completely straight, are they? Didn't you use a spirit level?'

She should have expected it! The word contrary must have been invented for Dr Fergus Browne!

'Actually, no,' she replied through gritted teeth.

'Perhaps you'd like me to take them down and start again?'

He raised his eyebrows. 'Don't be silly, I was only teasing! Would you get me a Dr Henry Burke at St Thomas's on the line? I'd like to speak to him.'

She did as he asked, and then he handed her a tape for the audio machine.

'I did this last night,' he explained. 'It has to be in as soon as possible, so can you give it priority.'

She nodded and took the tape, and the two of them worked in companionable silence for the next couple of hours, Poppy rattling away on the keyboard of the fairly new electric typewriter, and Dr Browne scribbling furiously.

When she presented him with the finished copy, he looked up with an expression of mild surprise on his face.

'That was quick,' he remarked.

Quick! She'd gone as fast as she could, but she knew she was slower than a lot of experienced secretaries. He really must have had some dud typists if he thought *she* was quick!

She glanced at her watch. It was almost half-past eleven.

'Excuse me, Dr Browne,' she began.

He looked up from the paper he was studying, the grey eyes focusing on her face as if she'd woken him from a trance.

'Yes? What is it?'

Poppy wished he wouldn't bark at her like that. 'I'm going to get myself a cup of coffee. Would you like one?'

'What? Oh, a coffee—yes, please.' He started reading again.

'Er—how do you like your coffee, Dr Browne?'

'What? Oh—black, no sugar.'

'And tea?'

He gave a click of annoyance. 'What is this—the Spanish Inquisition? Milk, no sugar in tea.'

'Thank *you*,' she said in an exaggeratedly patient voice. 'Now I know, and I shan't have to ask you again. Just one thing more, Dr Browne. . .'

'Oh, for goodness' sake! What is it now?'

'To fetch us a cup of coffee I have to walk all the way over to the canteen, which is a waste of time, and by the time I get it back here it will probably be cold. So I was wondering if I could bring a kettle in?'

He frowned. 'I don't see why not. Have you got a kettle to bring?'

'Oh, yes,' replied Poppy conversationally. 'When we got our new jug kettle to match the kitchen——' She stopped hastily when she saw the expression on his face, and remembered what he had said about not liking chit-chat. Miserable beast!

He was looking at her curiously. 'Are you always quite so outspoken and persistent?' he enquired.

It didn't *sound* like an insult, she thought cautiously, as she considered his question.

'I haven't been, up until now,' she explained. 'My last job didn't exactly encourage it.'

'Your last job being. . .?' he probed.

She was half inclined to tell him that he was now indulging in idle gossip, but on second thoughts. . .!

'I worked at Maxwells,' she told him.

'Maxwells? The department store in town?' He sounded surprised.

'The very same!'

'But not as a shop assistant, surely?'

She laughed. 'A glorified shop assistant. My official title was "beautician".'

'Beautician?' He had obviously never heard the word before. 'And what does a beautician do, pray?'

'She gets women to spend far too much money on make-up, that's what!'

A shaft of sunlight speared through a dispersing storm cloud, giving his eyes the appearance of the silvery mercury she'd once played with in a long-distant science lesson.

'I've never known anyone who's done *that* kind of work before,' he said in a bemused fashion.

She could imagine. 'Well, there's no need to say it like that—you make it sound as though I were a stripper!' she joked, and saw his eyes narrow. Oh, dear, had she gone too far? 'I'd better go and get our coffee,' she said hastily, and sped off.

Fergus sat perfectly still for a moment after the door had closed. The girl had all the life and vitality of an electrical storm. Had he perhaps bitten off more than he could chew by taking her on? She was far livelier than the usual temps the agency sent. He sighed as he picked up his pencil and resumed his paper.

Ten minutes later Poppy returned with the coffee and he drank his without seeming to notice what he was doing. After a couple of minutes he handed back the article she'd typed.

'Just a couple of mistakes,' he told her. 'But not many. I've marked them in pencil. Could you make sure this gets off today, and I'll dictate a covering letter when I get back from the wards?'

He paused in the doorway, noticing for the first time what exceptionally beautiful eyes she had, and what a strange colour they were. Purple almost— what did they call eyes that colour? Violet, that was it. Violet eyes, the colour of the soft pansies that grew all winter in his great sprawling garden.

Mentally he admonished himself—for heaven's sake, man, comparing his secretary's eyes to a flower—whatever next? He must get an early night in tonight—he had obviously been working much too hard.

Poppy looked up, slightly disconcerted to be in the full glare of his rather penetrating stare.

'Yes, Dr Browne?' she asked expectantly. 'Will there be anything else?'

He cleared his throat. 'Er—it does seem a little stilted if we continue to address each other so formally. Is Poppy your real name?'

Trust him to guess! She blushed. 'No. No, it's not.'

'And what name did your good mother give you?'

'Agnes Mary,' she muttered reluctantly, and saw a smile cross his lips.

'I suppose that means I'd better stick to Poppy,' he sighed. 'What a name!'

His hand was on the handle of the door when he

turned round. 'And you, of course, must call me
Fergus.' He gave her a brief nod and was gone, and
Poppy sat gazing blankly at the closed door.

'Good grief!' she said quietly, echoing the first
words he had ever spoken to her.

CHAPTER FOUR

THAT first week was not without its hiccups. Poppy soon discovered what it was about Dr Browne which had made so many of his secretaries leave in floods of tears—it was his great extremes of mood. When he was angry, he was angry with such a vehemence that it left you reeling. If something was not right then he let you know in no uncertain terms.

She found herself having to learn a bewildering array of new terms—it was almost like learning a different language. Things like Necrobiosis Lipoidica, Pityriasis Versacolor, Xanthoma, Actinic Keratosis and Melanocytic Naevi. She didn't have a clue how to spell them either, and didn't dare ask Dr Browne—or 'Fergus', as she was now supposed to call him!—for help. Instead, she bought herself a nurse's dictionary and scoured down lists of words until she found the dermatological term which most resembled what he had said!

Surprisingly there were few mistakes, but on her fourth morning he leapt up from his desk where he had been signing some letters which she had typed for him and thrust one of them under her nose.

'Just look at this!' he demanded, and she took the offending missive from him and read it, before turning her large violet eyes on him.

'What's wrong with it?' she asked, and he gave an indignant bark.

'What's *wrong* with it?' he exclaimed incredulously. 'You mean you don't even know?'

'If I did, then I wouldn't be asking you, would I?' she replied sweetly, and was rewarded with an angry glare.

'You have typed,' he said carefully, '"He was an Oriental, complacent person, and not on time."'

'And what's wrong with that?' she enquired, puzzled.

'Because, you woolly-headed individual, what I actually said was "He was orientated in place and person, but not in time."'

Poppy met his angry stare for a moment, and then to her horror began to giggle, and once she had started, she found it impossible to stop.

'Oh, I'm sorry,' she gasped eventually, wiping her eyes. 'I know I shouldn't laugh, and I'll re-type it straight away, but you have to admit, it is funny.'

For a split second she thought she saw his lips twitch, but on second thoughts she had probably imagined it.

'Hmm,' he muttered. 'Just try to *listen* to my tapes properly in future, won't you?'

So he could be extremely bad-tempered, but—and it was a big 'but'—he was without a doubt the most brilliantly gifted person she had ever met in her life, and this made her make allowances for his temper. The work he did just made the careers of every other man she had known seem so insignificant. How could somebody get so irritated at the progress of stocks and shares in the City, or about their latest advertising campaign, when this man was treating unsightly diseases and offering his patients some hope?

Fortunately she was a fast learner, and the odd mistake gradually disappeared. She felt she had come to terms with nearly all the most difficult medical terminology, and was working as hard as she could. For interest and involvement, the job beat Maxwells hands down.

She telephoned her friend and asked her if she could recommend any particular brand of cosmetic cover-up.

'Funnily enough, we've just had a new product in last month and it's brilliant. Why do you want to know?' asked Nicky.

Poppy explained about her boss's patient.

'Why don't you bring her into the shop, then, and we'll get to work on her?'

Poppy telephoned Ginny and arranged to take her down to Nicky's small beauty salon one evening after work. She was given a tube of the concealment foundation, and Poppy showed how best to apply it, using a damp sponge instead of her fingers as she had been doing. The transformation was startling.

And on the way home, Poppy was as tactful as possible when she spoke to the teenager.

'I think you look lovely with your new make-up on, but I think your attitude has a lot to do with how people are going to treat you at college,' she said.

'What do you mean?' asked the girl suspiciously.

'Well, if you're bright and sparky and refuse to be

cowed by your condition, then people are bound to respond to you more positively. If you don't become obsessed with your skin, then neither will they, they probably won't even really notice it that much, unless you bring it to their attention. If you don't feel sorry for yourself, then they won't feel sorry for you. Do you see what I mean?'

'I think so,' Ginny answered shyly. 'You're a brick, Poppy! Fergus has been looking for a decent secretary for *yonks*—thank goodness he's found one!'

Poppy found herself blushing in the darkness of the car, though she couldn't for the life of her imagine why.

After that, things seemed to go from being better, to being absolutely brilliant. In fact, her first month was a bit of a triumph, according to Miss Humphries, the motherly woman who was in charge of all the medical secretaries at Highchester Hospital. Poppy had been summoned to her office on the Friday morning and she went rather glumly, imagining that now she was going to be told politely that her services were no longer needed.

To her astonishment, Miss Humphries had said no such thing, quite the opposite, in fact.

'Do sit down, Miss Henderson,' she had smiled.

'Poppy,' she suggested winningly.

'Poppy, then.' When Poppy had settled herself, Miss Humphries surveyed the colourful young creature across her desk with a look of supreme relief on her face.

'I can't tell you how pleased I am, Poppy,' she began. 'Dr Browne has expressed no dissatisfaction with your work—so far, of course,' she added hastily, lest Poppy think she need be less diligent in future. 'In fact,' she confided, 'when I asked him how you were doing, he said "not bad".'

Poppy smiled.

'Not bad,' repeated Miss Humphries wonderingly. 'You may think those scant words of praise, Poppy, but, let me assure you, Dr Browne is not a man given to the superlative.' She began to wonder if she had been indiscreet. She did not want to put the girl off. 'Not that there's anything wrong with Dr Browne, of course,' she amended. 'A brilliant man—absolutely brilliant. And, like so many brilliant men, he can be difficult to work for.'

Difficult indeed. He was certainly the most unpredictable man that Poppy had ever met. When he was working, his attention was unwavering and woe betide anyone who tried to interrupt him. But then, just occasionally and without any warning, he would tease her or make a subtle joke and the light grey eyes would actually twinkle with humour.

But Poppy found it inexplicable that such an eminent man should dress like some hard-up student. And his *ties*—she'd never seen anything like them. He had spotty ones, tartan ones, even ones with small green hippos on them. Maybe they were cheap because no one else would be seen dead wearing them.

Perhaps he *was* hard up, she mused one morning as she slit open one envelope after another, all

addressed to him, all with the bewilderingly long list
of letters which always appeared after his name.
Perhaps he sent all his money to his ageing
parents. . .perhaps. . .

'Poppy!' he scowled, and she was taken aback to
see him towering over her desk, almost as if she had
magicked him up with her thoughts.

'If you've quite finished your little reverie,' he said
sarcastically, 'I said good morning to you twice, and
you didn't even hear me.'

'Sorry.' She beamed at him. 'Would you like some
coffee?'

He looked slightly mollified. 'Would I? I'd love
some. I had a review article to finish last night, and
I didn't get to bed until four this morning.'

She gave a little click of disapproval as she stirred
a great, strong steaming mugful of black coffee and
put it down on the desk in front of him. She had
used some money from petty cash to buy him a mug
which stated 'We all know who's the boss around
here!' and she had seen him laugh when he had first
read it.

He worked far too hard, of course. Often he
seemed in danger of forgetting about lunch completely, unless she silently disappeared to return
bearing a sandwich and a glass of juice, and some
fruit. She tried to get him the most nourishing
sandwich possible—cheese with salad, or tuna and
tomato. He was much too thin, she thought critically. But strong and wiry, all the same.

He never mentioned a wife. Surely a wife wouldn't
let him walk around looking like that? The shirts he

wore looked as though they had never seen an iron, and some of the cuffs were worn and faded. It's nothing to do with you, she told herself sternly. You're here to type his letters and answer the phone.

And this she did, but a lot more besides. The make-up sessions with Ginny proved a remarkable success, and even Fergus was astounded at the transformation. Ginny immediately wanted Poppy to show two of her friends who she'd met at one of Fergus's outpatients clinics how to apply the foundation. They were also afflicted with the disfiguring acne. Poppy, very flattered, agreed straight away, and again wrought such an improvement that she was contacted by a young woman with a particularly bad birthmark.

Even Fergus was impressed, and wanted to know how she did it.

'It can't just be this new product you're using, can it?—or there would have been more written up on it. So what's the secret?'

'Well, a lot of it's what beauticians call "styling",' she admitted.

'Styling?' He looked puzzled.

'Well, I *do* get them to apply the concealer with a damp sponge instead of fingertips, which definitely works better. But I also give them tips on their hairstyle and colour, and I point out that if they wear a lovely shawl, or an unusual brooch, and if they have co-ordinating accessories, the attention is drawn to the whole look rather than just the face, so the skin condition kind of loses some of its importance.'

'Clever girl!' he said admiringly, and she went pink.

After about a month, Fergus started sending people with newly diagnosed skin conditions up to his office to see Poppy, if he thought they could benefit from her expertise. For the first time in her life she felt as though she had a purpose. As if she were doing a job that counted, something important, something worthwhile.

One day Fergus happened to catch sight of a thick paperback sticking out from her basket.

'What's that you're reading?' he enquired idly.

She blushed. 'It's called *The Ragged-Trousered Philanthropists*.'

'Tressell,' he murmured. 'What on earth are you doing reading that?'

'Why shouldn't I?' she retorted.

'Oh, I think it's commendable,' he said hastily. 'It's just that I'm rather surprised, that's all. I suppose I expected you to have a love story or something, that's what the girls usually bring.'

'What a cheek!' she exclaimed indignantly. 'Do you think that education stops once you've grown up? Or perhaps you believe that only people who go to university have a monopoly on decent literature? I happen to belong to a book club, and every fortnight we meet to discuss the book we've all been reading—and this is our latest choice. And I'm enjoying it very much indeed!'

'Sorry, Poppy,' he said humbly. 'I shouldn't have tried to pigeonhole you.'

'No, you shouldn't!' she agreed, and walked over to the filing cabinet. 'Love story, indeed!'

He watched her flounce across the office—more to make a point than out of pique, he thought, and found himself gazing at her long legs in the short skirt she wore. She really *was* gorgeous, he thought, and hastily began writing about Lichen Planus in an effort to banish his thoughts.

And Poppy found herself wondering why, no matter how foul he could be to her, she didn't seem to care.

But she was learning all the time. Just through typing his letters she gleaned all kinds of knowledge about Fergus's chosen speciality of dermatology.

She learned that twenty per cent of all new patients referred to his clinics were suffering from eczema, or dermatitis as it used to be called. And that dermatology dealt with conditions as varying as psoriasis, seborrhoeic warts, ringworm and scabies to disturbing and sometimes fatal conditions such as epidermolysis bullosa and malignant melanoma.

He had heaps of books with colour plates showing disfiguring and debilitating skin eruptions, and when she had a rare quiet moment in the office, Poppy found herself reading the simpler ones. It seemed that the more she learnt about his work, then the more interesting her job became.

October was colder than usual, with early fierce winds that brutally ripped the leaves from the trees. One morning Poppy overslept. There was no time for make-up, no time to curl her hair, or even to eat breakfast. On the way to work she got thoroughly soaked and had to hang her dripping outer garments near the blazing radiator in the office. Her hair had started to turn to frizz, so she tied it back in a simple ponytail.

She was busy sorting through the post when Fergus arrived, and he stood stock still in the middle of the room, staring at her.

'*You* look nice this morning,' he commented, throwing his briefcase in the corner of the room. She did too. All that hair scraped off her face meant that you could see her extraordinarily fine bone structure. And the violet eyes, unadorned by that muck she usually wore, looked huge and quite stunning.

She glared at him. Sarcastic beast. 'Ha, ha—very funny,' she retorted. 'I haven't had a chance to do my hair or my face, and I got drenched on the way here!'

'Hmm. Maybe you should do that more often,' he observed wryly, before pulling the *British Journal of Dermatology* towards him.

She was irritated by his words, but they set her thinking. Just recently she had started to realise that perhaps the way she looked *was* a bit over the top. And it seemed kind of inappropriate in the hospital setting. At Maxwells all the girls who worked there had gone to town with cosmetics and the like, but here she was aware that she stuck out like a sore thumb. It was much further to get to work in the mornings than it had been at Maxwells, so she had to leave the flat earlier. Suddenly, spending ages carefully applying eye-liner had begun to lose its appeal. For the first time in her life it actually seemed a waste of time.

That weekend she went to her hairdresser.

'The usual, is it?' he asked, giving her his cheeky grin. 'Roots touching up and a trim?'

Poppy looked at her reflection in the mirror, at the pale blonde hair that tumbled down over her shoulders in a mass of carefully curled ringlets.

'I want to grow the colour out,' she announced.

Roni's eyebrows almost disappeared. 'You're kidding?'

'No, I'm not. I want to grow the colour out, and I want a change—what do you suggest?'

According to Roni, the best thing to do about the colour would be to tint her hair to her natural colour, so that it could grow out slowly. But first he cut it. . .

Two hours later Poppy stared in astonishment at her image. Gone was the marshmallow girl of earlier. Her hair fell in a superbly cut glossy bob, just to her chin. The shining golden-brown hair emphasised the amazing eyes, just as nature had intended it to. Roni gave a huge smile.

'Wow! If I say so myself, I've done a magnificent job! You look—oh, I don't know—you look chic. Different. Almost French—if your hair were darker. Are you pleased, Poppy?'

Pleased? She was delighted. And Ella almost didn't recognise her, or so she said.

'You'll have to buy a few classic pieces now, to go with your sophisticated new image!' she declared.

'Sophisticated? Who—me? Never!' laughed

Poppy, but it set her thinking. Next pay day maybe
she would buy something a little different.

She and Ella went to the pub that evening—their
old stomping ground. Mick Douglas was there, but
got no joy out of Poppy when he enquired whether
she was still working for the hot-headed maniac.

Julian Bell was there as well. He worked in
advertising, drove the obligatory Porsche and had a
flat in town. He had taken Poppy out to supper once
and then a nightclub, but he had such ghastly
wandering hands that she had declined any further
invitations, though she had remained friendly. The
trouble was that Julian was one of those men who,
once rejected, felt that they must do everything in
their power to make the woman change her mind.
But Poppy was used to Julian, and immune to his
charms.

Towards the end of the evening everyone seemed
to be having a good time, playing a silly version of 'I
spy', but Poppy sat on the outskirts of the circle,
feeling oddly ill at ease. She felt like an outsider, as
if she'd outgrown the crowd. They seemed to think
no further than about where the next drink was
coming from. Suddenly the jokes she had once
laughed at seemed trite. She shook her head. She
wondered what Fergus was doing. Reading some
confounded article, she'd bet. Probably hadn't
remembered to eat his supper.

She felt an overwhelming desire to make a wish.
That she was spending the evening with Fergus,
cooking him a stew rich with wine and herbs while
he worked. And after they had eaten they would sit

down with their coffee and she could tell him all
about the book she'd just read, and they could
discuss social deprivation in the last century. . .

'Are you all right, Poppy?'

'What?' She realised that Julian was talking to
her, a question in those lazy eyes. 'Yes, I'm fine.'
With a stiff, jerky movement she reached her hand
out and grabbed the glass of dry Martini, taking a
large sip to hide her discomfiture.

She was behaving like an overgrown schoolgirl.
There was no point in someone like her dreaming of
someone like him. He was way out of her league.
She was a typist, when it boiled down to it—and
Fergus was a consultant, one of the top specialists in
his field.

No point in imagining herself to be half in love
with him, because that was a silly, foolish dream.

And everyone knew that dreams did not come
true.

CHAPTER FIVE

FERGUS was in a good mood—she could tell. After two months of working for the man, Poppy felt she knew him very well—not that he had ever told her anything about himself. He had adhered strictly to his own rule of not indulging in 'chit-chat'. She knew he was in a good mood because he had forgotten to put one of his revolting ties on, and resembled a hard-up student even more than usual.

He beamed at her as he strode into the office, his tall, angular frame bending over her desk, disconcertingly close as he slapped a bulky-looking envelope down in front of her.

'It's finished!' he announced proudly.

She blinked at him. 'What is?'

'My manuscript. I've written a new book.'

She blinked again. 'A book? That's marvellous!'

'They may not like it,' he pondered. 'But they did commission it, so there shouldn't be a problem. There's just one small thing. . .'

'Yes, Fergus?' She smiled. He was about to lay the charm on, and his charm was the one thing she could not resist.

'It'll need typing. . .and I wondered if you could do it for me? I'll pay you extra, of course.'

'Of course I'll type it.' Now, she thought. Ask him

now. 'Um—you know your grand ward round on Wednesdays?' she began.

'My ward round?' He looked a little lost. 'Yes? What about it?'

It all came out in one breathless, over-rehearsed rush. 'Well, you know that your patients often telephone you here, or sometimes they even come in to see you, and they don't have a clue who I am, and vice versa. And you know you're always saying how important continuity is for patients, particularly those who are insecure, as so many of yours are. . .'

'So I do.' She had his total interest now.

'Well, I thought that if I could come on your grand ward round with you, then I'd get to know them. . .' Her voice faded away in embarrassment. 'I wouldn't neglect my work to do it; I could always stay late to finish my typing on that evening.'

'And is that the only reason why you want to come?' he asked softly.

She glanced at him quickly—don't say he had guessed she had developed a stupid infantile crush on him? No, he couldn't have—she valued her job far too much to ever let that show.

'Actually, yes. There is another reason. I happen to find the work—your work, that is—very interesting.'

He nodded. 'I thought so.' He walked over to his desk. 'Shall I tell you what my old chemistry master used to say to me?'

She nodded.

'He used to tell us that enthusiasm was the most precious human quality. That without it man would have discovered very little. You've got great enthusiasm, Poppy—which is what makes you the best secretary I've ever had, and yes, I should be delighted for you to accompany me on the ward round on Wednesdays.'

She went pink all round the back of her neck at his words. Fulsome praise from Dr Browne, indeed!

That Wednesday she walked with him to his ward, which was situated in the vast gleaming new block of the hospital. The ward itself was nothing how she had imagined it. She had envisaged a long, dark old-fashioned place with curtained beds on either side of a central aisle, but she could not have been more wrong. There were four patients to each cubicle.

'That way we hope to eliminate as much cross-infection as possible,' explained Fergus. 'Which is important on every ward, but especially so among patients who might have open lesions.'

There was a man in charge of the ward, which also surprised her, and whom Fergus introduced as Geoff, the charge nurse. She met the rest of the team, which was very small, but then dermatology was one of the smaller specialities.

Mr Khan was Fergus's registrar, a small, gentle man whom Poppy had met once or twice when he'd been asking Fergus for advice on an examination he was due to take next month.

'And this is James West,' said Fergus. 'I don't believe you've met yet?'

No, she certainly hadn't met James West before. She would have remembered meeting someone who looked like *that*. He was almost indecently good-looking—big, broad shoulders and a tanned, smiling face in which blazing blue eyes twinkled. Crisp blond curls completed the Greek god-like image, and he held his hand out to grasp hers, holding it in his own for just slightly too long.

He had the kind of looks that ninety per cent of the female population would have swooned over, but Poppy was not one of them. She found herself comparing his muscular bulk to the wiry, angular frame of her boss, the bright fair curls to the lock of brown hair which always seemed to flop over Fergus's eye, and the blue eyes to those narrow grey ones which so rarely lit up with pleasure but when they did were brighter than the brightest jewel.

'Delighted,' he murmured. 'No wonder Fergus has been hiding you away in his office!'

She waited for Fergus to bite his head off, but to her slight annoyance he didn't even appear to have heard his houseman's comment; he was busy scribbling something in a set of notes which Geoff had handed to him.

What was she hoping he would do? Leap over and place his arm protectively around her shoulder while telling James not to be so familiar with his secretary? There was nothing wrong with being a little bit in love with her boss, she reasoned, just so long as she understood that it was always going to be unrequited.

Fergus had finished writing. He glanced up and smiled absently. 'You've all met Poppy now—she wants to come round with us every Wednesday, so I hope you'll answer any questions she may have.'

They began their slow passage around the ward, and the first thing that struck Poppy was what awful conditions people had to live with.

They had stopped before a bed on which lay a middle-aged man whose skin was covered in what looked like small yellow bumps.

Mr Khan began to speak. 'This patient presented to his general practitioner and routine examination of blood and urine showed that he is suffering from diabetes mellitus. On seeing the small yellowish papules, his GP decided to refer him to us for tests. His diagnosis is one of eruptive xanthoma.'

Fergus nodded. 'Thanks, Khan. Are we having him examined for sites of predilection for other xanthomas?'

'We're fasting him tonight.'

'And do you know what we'll be checking for, James?' enquired Fergus.

James had been too busy staring at the long, slim column of Poppy's neck on to which the shiny hair hung like a neat cap. Why hadn't he seen her around the place before?'

'Er—no—sorry, Fergus, haven't come across it before.'

'We'll be checking the blood cholesterol, trihlycer-ides and lipoprotein profile, and enquiring closely into family history of ischaemic heart disease. And of course we'll treat the diabetes.'

Fergus perched on the edge of the man's chair.

'How are you feeling today, Mr Handsworth?' he asked.

The man perked up. 'A lot better than when they brought me in, Doctor! When do you reckon I'll be home?'

Fergus smiled. 'I think in a day or two when we've completed all our tests, and when the dietician has been to see you again. Has anyone explained to you about your diabetes?'

Mr Handsworth nodded. 'The young doctor there did.'

James grinned. 'That's the first time I've been called young in ages—thanks, Mr Handsworth!'

They all laughed and the round moved on. Poppy found it very distressing to see a young man whose lips were completely congealed with unsightly, blistering lesions.

Fergus again moved up close to the patient, and Poppy remembered something he had written. 'Relatively few dermatological disorders are infectious, although from an uninformed point of view they may look it. Therefore, close contact with the patient can be useful to reinforce the idea that they should not expect to be ostracised, and it is up to hospital staff to lead the way'.

'Hello, Johnny. Would you like to know what you've got?' he said.

Johnny nodded dismally. 'I suppose so.'

'It's called erythema multiforma and we've traced it back to those drugs you were given—remember the salphonamides you had? We've made a note on your records that you're allergic to them, and the

good news is that the lesions should fade fairly
quickly.'

Johnny gave a wide smile. 'Thank God for that! I
was terrified that my girlfriend would never kiss me
again!'

Fergus gave a laugh at this, and Poppy found
herself wondering, not for the first time, whether
there was anyone special in Fergus Browne's life.
She had been working for him for eight weeks and
in all that time he had received no personal calls at
the office. Perhaps he had a girlfriend and he bossed
her around mercilessly, forbidding her to contact
him except in an emergency. Maybe he even banned
what he loved to call 'chit-chat' on their dates
together!

They all congregated in Sister's office afterwards,
where James managed to get Poppy by herself in a
corner.

'So why haven't I seen you around the hospital
before now?' He gave her the benefit of his dazzling
smile. 'Have you been working for Fergus for long?'

'Only about eight weeks,' she replied, accepting a
cup of tea from Geoff, the charge nurse, and carefully adding some milk to the cup. 'I tend to work
through my lunch-hour—and the canteen is a bit of
a trudge.'

'I have the perfect solution—let's have a picnic
nearer your office?' suggested James.

Poppy laughed. 'A picnic? In this weather? Is your
real name Scott of the Antarctic?'

James eyed her thoughtfully. 'Well, some day

when you're not so busy, then? Let me buy you
lunch—surely you can't have any objection to that?'

Of course she didn't have, and why on earth
should she? She was a free agent. Did she imagine
that Fergus Browne had some kind of proprietorial
claim over her?

'All right,' she agreed. 'Give me a ring some
time.'

'Done!' He swallowed the last of his tea. 'I'd
better get going now—too many notes to write
before this poor medic can knock off! I'll be seeing
you, Poppy.'

'Goodbye.' She watched him leave, still sipping
her tea, totally unaware that Fergus had been watching closely, had heard the entire conversation, and
had nodded very slightly when he heard Poppy agree
to have lunch with his houseman. Almost as if
something which he had been expecting to happen
had finally happened.

CHAPTER SIX

THE Wednesday ward round began to be the high point of Poppy's week. It seemed to draw all the different threads of her job together to form the complete picture. Because Fergus's work was primarily, as for all doctors, about patients—and Poppy realised that her job would seem much emptier without the weekly contact with those patients.

Suddenly a name in a GP's letter asking for an opinion became a face, and the face had a family and a home! Poppy soon discovered that bringing someone into hospital wasn't always just an isolated incident, a simple task. Old people living on their own might have a cat, and who would feed the cat while they were away? A mother might have two small children—who would look after them? Could the father get compassionate leave? If someone's eczema had been caused because they were allergic to some substance in the factory where they worked, then how easy was it going to be for them to find a new job? Poppy began to understand how important the much-maligned social worker's role was.

She began to get to know all the different staff who worked on the wards—the ward clerk, the people who cleaned the ward, the League of Friends who brought round the daily newspaper and toiletries trolley and who did so much more besides.

Then there were all the different grades of nurses, the physiotherapists, the pharmacist, the radiographer, the dietician—the list went on and on!

One Wednesday there was a clutch of medical students attached to the round. One arrived chewing gum, which immediately caused Fergus to bawl at him. That the student seemed uninterested in the round would have been an understatement, to say the least; in fact Poppy thought all three of them were pretty dozy. She could see Fergus's temper getting shorter and shorter, and the atmosphere was getting more strained by the minute.

They all trooped into the office, and after a series of questions which all drew blank responses, Fergus finally snapped.

'Just what *do* they teach you these days?' he roared. 'Doesn't *anyone* know the treatment for Rosacea?'

There was a deathly hush. Shoes were studied, the pattern of the floor seemed to take on enormous significance to most of those present. Not one of them looked Fergus in the face. Except Poppy. They stared very hard at one another.

'Oxytetracyclin,' she said calmly, and you could have heard a pin drop.

'What?'

'Oxytetracyclin,' she repeated, 'is usually effective as a treatment for Rosacea. Erythromycin as a second choice.'

She heard Geoff draw his breath in, saw Mr Khan's shoulders shake.

For a long moment Fergus regarded her steadily,

then he threw back his head and laughed. 'Now who says I haven't got the best secretary in the hospital?' he chuckled.

Her workload gradually increased. Apart from typing up reports, typing referrals, taking telephone calls, she was given the added responsibility of organising a dermatology conference which was to be held in the hospital. Fergus had asked her about it rather uncertainly one morning.

'Would you mind?' he asked. 'I know I give you a lot of work to do, but. . .' The light grey eyes met hers appealingly, and to Poppy the most astonishing thing about him was that he was completely oblivious of the charm he exercised. If he had asked her to be fired from a cannon to the moon, she was pretty sure that the answer would be yes.

She smiled and nodded. 'You know I don't mind—I'm a pushover for hard work!'

He gave one of his rare relaxed grins. 'You're turning out to be Wonder Woman—if you knew how much easier you've made my life. . .

And if he only knew how he had eaten into hers!

She booked the conference hall, after checking that the eight—including Fergus—main speakers were free on that day. She had invitations printed and distributed to all the leading hospitals in the country, inviting not only dermatologists themselves, but in some cases consultant physicians who had a special interest in dermatology.

She spoke to one of the drug companies, one that manufactured Fergus's favourite type of steroid cream, used for the treatment of eczema. The drug company agreed to sponsor the conference, in return for the use of a stand outside the main hall, which would carry leaflets about the drug and samples for the doctors to try. In return they would provide lunch for two hundred, morning coffee and afternoon tea.

Apart from the extra work of the conference, Poppy continued to struggle with the manuscript of his book, and struggle was certainly the operative word. He had written it in longhand, in his crazy flowing style which resembled a spider that had dipped its feet in a bottle of ink and then staggered across the paper. Some words she recognised simply because she had typed them so often, therefore Pso. . .followed by a drunken-looking squiggle she knew was the word psoriasis, and likewise she worked out words such as 'excoriated' and 'seborrhoeic'. When she was really stuck, she quietly moved across to his desk to ask him, when, depending if he was engrossed in a piece of writing, he would as often as not snap at her.

She learnt to take no notice of this and to mildly repeat the question, for which she would be rewarded with the answer, accompanied by a ferocious glare.

Once, when he had been in an especially good mood, she had taken him to task about his methods of writing.

'Can't you type with two fingers, and get it all down on a word processor?' she asked.

'That's what you get paid for,' he growled.

'Well, why can't you dictate it on to your dicta-phone, and I can type it—it would make it much easier.'

'Easier for you, maybe. It wouldn't help *me* any. I need to see what it looks like on the page before I know if it's going to work. And now, if you've quite finished trying to ram technology down my throat. . .'

Poppy gave a loud, huffy sigh—which naturally went unheard by her crusty boss. Never, never had she met a man quite like him!

Sometimes she didn't return to the flat until past eight o'clock and Ella, her flatmate, had begun to take her to task.

'Just what's going on, Poppy? Do you have a secret rendezvous most evenings, or is there more to this relationship with the mysterious Fergus than you're prepared to tell me?'

Poppy blushed a deep red and poured herself a cup of coffee. 'Don't be so ridiculous—he's not even there half the time. I'm just busy with his book, and the conference, and lots of things.'

Ella gave her a disapproving stare. 'I just hope you're working for money, not love.'

Poppy forced a smile. 'Honestly, Ella, you'd see a romance anywhere, even where none existed!'

'Speaking of romance,' Ella butted in eagerly, 'Julian keeps on asking where you've been lately.'

'Julian?' Poppy turned her mouth down at the corners. 'You know I can't stand him, he's got a bad case of the wandering hands!'

'Well, what about that doctor from the hospital,

the one you said they all think is dishy, who keeps asking you out? Why won't you go?'

'I've been too busy, and too tired,' protested Poppy. 'I may go out with him some time, but he's not my type.'

'Then hand him over to me!' Ella paused. 'Julian was just saying the other evening that we never seem to see you much these days, and that when we do you're so incredibly serious that you're no fun to be with. He said he loves your new hairstyle and your new look, but he wishes he could have the old Poppy back.'

'Oh, does he?' snapped Poppy furiously. 'Well, tell Julian that I just became tired of being the perpetual clown, that's all. I love my job and I'm very happy at the moment—and I'm surprised that you and Julian haven't got anything better to talk about than me!' She turned away from her flatmate and began to chop viciously at a cucumber.

What was it about Fergus Browne that so captivated her? He was bad-tempered, crusty and a slave to his work. But his nature was like the colour of those enticing silvery eyes—mercurial. Underneath his often dour exterior there was humour, and a great deal of compassion.

Let's face it, she thought glumly as she tossed the cucumber in the bowl to join the peppers and the endive, the one main drawback about Fergus in her eyes was the fact that he might find her indispensable as a secretary, but she didn't even rate a second glance as a woman he might like to get to know better. . . She sighed. Maybe next week she *would* have lunch with James West.

She listened to the news headlines while she munched through her supper and then settled down with the latest book which the club had set for them to read. But it gave her no pleasure tonight to read the great classic *Jane Eyre*—the parallels between the relationship of Mr Rochester and Jane and her own with Fergus dominated all her thoughts, so that she almost jumped out of the chair when she heard unearthly screams, until, laughing nervously at her gullibility, she realised that the sound came from the television set, where Ella sat engrossed in a thriller.

'It's all arranged,' she told him with a beam of achievement.

Fergus looked up at her and blinked, a bemused expression on his face. 'Sorry?'

'It's all arranged,' Poppy repeated patiently.

'Arranged? What are you talking about? Who's arranged what?'

'The conference, Fergus—the blessed conference. You know, the one subject which has been dominating my typewriter and engaging the telephone line for weeks. The dermatology conference! It's taking place on January the fourteenth. Just thought you'd like to know.'

He put his pen down, pushed back the errant lock of hair on his forehead and smiled. 'That's terrific! Have you really sorted it all out? You're a very clever girl!'

Her latest policy was to completely block out the

odd crumb of praise which he threw in her direction; it only gave rise to a rapid heartbeat and disturbed nights while she lay there pondering on what he might really have meant.

She sat down at her desk and began re-reading the letters she had just finished typing, before presenting them to him for his signature, when he glanced up.

He was trying very hard not to concentrate on how splendid she looked in the soft jersey dress of jade green, thinking that it provided the ideal background for those incredible eyes. It was actually quite distracting sometimes, having someone sitting opposite him for most of the day who looked as though she should be gracing the pages of *Vogue*. Thank goodness Catherine was coming back.

He cleared his throat. 'Er—Poppy?'

'Yes, Fergus?'

'I was just wondering whether you'd tried to get in touch with Paul Burke?'

'Who?'

'He's a leading dermatologist—we were at medical school together.'

Poppy began flicking through her list of speakers. 'No, there's no one here of that name. Which hospital is he at?'

He looked rather sheepish. 'He practises in the States now.'

She raised her eyebrows. 'Well, actually—believe it or not, I haven't quite had the time to contact dermatologists internationally, though if you could arrange for me to have ninety hours of work in the week, instead of——'

He held his hand up. 'OK, I take your point. But do you think we could contact him, just him—no one else abroad? He's a great friend, *and* a professor—and you've always wanted to meet a professor, haven't you?' His eyes were twinkling and she knew that he was remembering their very first encounter.

'He's is also,' he informed her gravely, 'the person responsible for sending me the ties I know you're so fond of!'

She looked up quickly and they both burst out laughing. If she thought she had grown to know Fergus, then it seemed he was beginning to know her too.

'I'll get on to it right away,' she promised. 'Have we his phone number on file?'

He nodded and pointed to his personal book. 'Thanks,' he said briefly.

Poppy realised that Paul Burke was probably still sleeping, as his area of America was six hours behind them. She would ring him this afternoon.

She had picked up the letters again when the phone on her desk began to ring. 'Dr Browne's office,' she replied fluidly.

As soon as she heard the voice, her heart sank. Intelligent, attractively husky, well-modulated and, most of all breezing with self-assurance.

'Hello. Is Fergus around, please?'

'Who's calling, please?' trilled Poppy, far more officiously than her usual friendly manner.

'It's Catherine Bennett,' replied the voice confidently. Confident that he would speak to her, of course.

Poppy somehow knew. She called over to Fergus, 'It's Catherine Bennett—will you take the call?'

She didn't want to look at him, to see the smiling pleasure cross his face, yet some masochistic streak forced her to look, and she stared at him helplessly as he nodded, and she put the call through to him.

Poppy bent her head over her work, her mind registering every word he spoke.

'Catherine!' he exclaimed delightedly. 'When did you get back?'

He tipped his head to one side as he listened to her reply, a deep smile etched on to the perfect mouth.

'How about lunch?' he was saying. Another pause. 'Well, how about today, or are you too jet-lagged?'

Whatever she said made him laugh loudly, and Poppy was appalled by the unreasonable wave of jealousy which ran through her body.

'I'll see you at one, then. Come straight up—you can meet Poppy.' He looked up and smiled at Poppy indulgently. 'What? Yes, the name really suits her. What? Yes, she's my new secretary.'

And there she had it in a nutshell. She was his secretary, no more and no less. Of course he had someone—a man with the looks and the brains of Fergus Browne would be bound to have someone.

Fergus put the phone down, and smiled. 'That was Catherine,' he said unnecessarily.

'So I gathered.' Poppy struggled to keep the starchiness out of her voice. 'You've never mentioned her before.'

He looked surprised. 'No, of course I haven't. Why should I?'

Ouch! That had certainly put her in her place. 'No reason,' she said, forcing a lightness into her voice which she was far from feeling. 'Is she your girlfriend?'

He looked doubtful. 'I don't really like that expression—and besides, Catherine is a woman, hardly a girl.'

And he had called Poppy a 'clever girl' that morning. When would she ever learn?

'I suppose you might call her that,' he said doubtfully. 'We've known each other for a long time.'

Well, bully for you! she felt like shouting unreasonably at him, but she gave a small, cold smile instead.

'Do you mind if I go off early to lunch today?' she asked.

A look of disappointment crossed his face. 'Oh, must you? Can't you stay and see Catherine? I know she'd love to meet you.'

I bet she would, thought Poppy grimly. And if I were going out with a man like Fergus I'd want to vet his secretaries too.

'I'd love to,' she lied. 'But I've promised my flatmate that I'd meet her. I'll have to go when I've finished this letter.'

She began to type furiously, banging her fingers down hard on the keyboard, and inevitably she began to make mistakes. Fergus saw the Tippex bottle being opened for the third time and glanced up, mildly surprised.

'Why we can't have a self-correcting typewriter, I *don't* know,' she grumbled.

Now he *was* surprised. Poppy was many things—honest to a fault, outspoken and highly adaptable. So why had she started moaning about the typewriter? Previously she had assured him that she was perfectly happy with it.

'We're stuck with that one,' he laughed, 'for exactly the same reason why we're entombed in this dilapidated building, and why, if you weren't working through the agency, you'd be earning next to nothing.'

'Hmph,' she grunted, and began to clatter away again.

What was the matter with her? he wondered. Surely her nose hadn't been put out of joint by the imminent arrival of Catherine. Oh, for heaven's sake Fergus, he chided himself, are you getting early-onset dementia? As if Poppy Henderson—bright young Poppy with her beautiful big violet eyes and her winning smile—would ever be interested in a bad-tempered, crusty academic like himself!

Let me out of here, prayed Poppy silently as she typed in BA, MD, FRCP next to his name. Let me out of here before I make a gigantic fool of myself by bursting into tears. She scrambled to her feet, grabbing her coat and handbag, and then the door opened.

The best laid plans of mice and men, she thought ruefully, as she stood with a fixed smile on her face to confront the elegant woman she knew was Catherine Bennett.

She was scarcely aware of Fergus jumping to his feet, the introductions he made, or even the fact that he had planted a kiss on Catherine's smooth cheek. All she could think of was how she could have imagined that Fergus might ever be interested in her, when he had someone like the elegant creature who stood opposite her.

She was quite small—no, small was the wrong word entirely. She was petite. Dainty. She made Poppy feel like a gawky, leggy young foal. She had glossy hair as black as soot, and large velvet brown eyes. She wore a classic linen suit of a pale, pinky-grey colour, with not a crease in sight, and the slim black patent clutch bag she carried under her arm exactly matched the shiny court shoes. She was smiling at Poppy, and the smile reached her eyes.

'Hello, Poppy,' she said, holding out her hand. 'I'm very pleased to meet you.'

And that in its way was the worst possible thing—she seemed so nice that Poppy couldn't help warming to her. How much easier it would have been had Catherine eyed her suspiciously, her dark eyes flashing fire. If she had looked her up and down in an openly hostile way, nothing would have pleased Poppy more. Because then she would have felt as if it were somehow OK to continue liking him the way she did. But Catherine was not like that, and it was definitely not OK.

'I'm pleased to meet you too,' she managed to say, returning the woman's handshake.

'Poppy's meeting a friend—otherwise I'd have invited her to join us,' interjected Fergus, his hand pushing back the lock of hair in that unconsciously schoolboyish gesture.

Catherine looked genuinely disappointed. 'Oh, what a shame! Never mind—I'm sure we'll run into each other again.'

'I'm sure we will,' said Poppy as she headed for the door. 'Goodbye, it was nice to have met you.'

'Bye!'

She almost ran along the draughty corridor, half afraid that they might follow her out, that she would be forced to watch them linking arms, or openly kissing.

I'm damn sure I wouldn't want to share our first lunch together if I were her, she thought fiercely, before reason flooded back into her mind. You've got to stop it, Poppy, she told herself. He's your boss. He's got Catherine. Your foolish little dreams have got to be terminated—and now!

There was no flatmate to meet, no hunger in her empty stomach. She pulled her overcoat close to her body and spent the hour walking, tramping over the fallen leaves and looking up with troubled eyes at the vast empty space of the cloudless sky.

CHAPTER SEVEN

THAT walk seemed to last for a very long time. As Poppy strode unseeingly through the mud and the leaves, she kept telling herself how ridiculous she was being. Why shouldn't Fergus have a girlfriend? And just what had she been expecting?

But it seemed that she could tell herself she was ridiculous until she was blue in the face, because it did nothing to ease the awful ache which had been present somewhere above where she imagined her stomach to be, since she had discovered dark, beautiful Catherine's existence.

Fergus must have had an unusually long lunch— well, naturally—because he didn't come back to the office, and she knew he had an outpatients' clinic which often didn't finish until nearly six. Usually she waited for him and he might make them both a cup of coffee while she typed out any of the really urgent documents which he wanted to get off straight away.

But today she couldn't face seeing him. Couldn't face him fidgeting around, not offering to make coffee for them—dying to rush away to meet his Catherine. And she didn't even give her theories a chance to be tested, because she went off at five-thirty, only the second occasion she had done that since she had first started there.

When Ella arrived home at the flat she saw Poppy sitting in the middle of the floor of a cold room.

'Brr!' she exclaimed, rubbing her hands together. 'It's absolutely freezing in here. Why haven't you put the heating on?'

Poppy looked up, startled, worlds away, her ears registering what her friend had said to her, and to both their amazement huge salt tears began to slide down her cheeks.

'Poppy!' cried Ella, alarmed now. 'My dear girl, whatever is the matter?'

'Nothing,' sniffed Poppy, in a barely recognisable tone, then she threw her arms around Ella's neck and began to cry like a child.

Ella let her cry for a bit, feeling absolutely perplexed. The two girls had shared a flat together for nearly two years, they were very close friends—and yet she could never remember seeing Poppy in anything resembling this state.

'Poppy, what's the matter with you? Can't you stop crying for a minute and tell me?'

'There's no point!' wailed Poppy.

Ella began to brighten up a bit. If Poppy was leaving her morose state to move on to one of her more dramatic moods, then things surely couldn't be *that* bad? She watched as she began to dab at her red-rimmed eyes with a paper handkerchief.

'You need a drink,' she announced.

Poppy nodded. 'I think I do.'

There wasn't very much in the flat. If they had a bottle they tended to drink it, and if there was more than a bottle, they threw a party. After much

searching and scrabbling around in the bottom of a
very dated bureau-cum-bookcase which helped com-
prise their 'furnished' accommodation, Ella managed to produce two dusty bottles, one containing
Amaretto, a delicious but rather sickly almond
liqueur which she had brought back from her pack-
age holiday in Italy, the other an unopened flask of
Spanish brandy.

'Let's have this,' she suggested.

'It's a bit rough,' sniffed Poppy doubtfully.

'Rubbish! We've got some fizzy mineral water in
the fridge—my father always drinks brandy and
soda!'

Poppy allowed herself to be given a generous
glassful of the so-called brandy and soda, and at
least the ice anaesthetised her lips a litle. A couple
of glassfuls and she was definitely feeling no pain.
Just an empty feeling if she cared to think about
Fergus Browne. And she didn't care. To think about
him, that was.

But unfortunately Ella was not a person given to
considering other people's finer feelings. Warmed
and emboldened by her equally generous slurps of
brandy, she launched straight into an interrogation.

'Come on now, Poppy, why the tears? I've known
you for over two years and I've never seen you like
this before. Spill the beans, for goodness' sake!'

Poppy shook her head. 'There's no point—it's
hopeless.'

'Rubbish! Confession is good for the soul!'
declared Ella.

'I don't think so, not in this case.' Poppy took

another sip, then quickly put the glass down. It was beginning to make her feel woozy on an empty stomach. She liked Ella—they had been close friends for a long time now. And wouldn't it be nice to unburden herself to someone?

'You mustn't tell anyone,' she began.

Ella sighed. 'Poppy, you can trust me—you know you can.'

'It's Fergus,' Poppy blurted out. 'I think I'm half in love with the man.'

A smile spread over Ella's features. 'Is that all? I've known that for weeks, you daft idiot. So why all the tears?'

'Because he's going out with someone called Catherine. I met her today.'

'Oh, dear! Is it serious?'

Poppy nodded. 'Apparently. They've known each other for a long time, so he told me. Then he took her out to lunch. And the trouble is that I liked her. She's lovely—pretty, friendly, self-assured. All the things that I'm not,' she finished moodily.

'Stop fishing for compliments! And anyway, how you look has nothing to do with it if he's already got a girlfriend. The question is—what are you intending to do about it?'

Poppy looked slightly alarmed. 'Do? What do you mean, do? There's nothing I can do.'

Ella topped their glasses up. 'Of course there is! Don't tell me you're intending to stay there, eating your heart out, mooning great big cow eyes at him every time he gives you a letter to type?'

'I do *not* moon over him!' declared Poppy heatedly. 'He has no idea how I feel.'

'I'd be very surprised if he hadn't,' murmured Ella sagely. 'What I'm saying is that surely you aren't considering staying on to work with him?'

'What are you talking about?'

Ella sighed. 'Just that you ought to be thinking about leaving, that's all.'

'Leave him?' Poppy exclaimed in horror. 'Leave Fergus? I couldn't do that, Ella—he needs me.'

Ella laughed. 'Needs you? What absolute poppycock—if you'll excuse the pun. Are you planning to become one of those joke figures, then? Refusing dates and living like a nun? Working long hours for this ghostly figure who already has someone else?

'And then what happens? He'll get married, and you, as the little secretary, will be invited. And you'll stand at the reception, a little drunk and on your own, slightly away from everyone else. Because of course you won't know anyone—you won't have met his friends because you're not part of his circle. You're just faithful old Poppy who types his letters. And you'll end up as some lonely old spinster, still pining after him in a way that's become slightly pathetic, while he carries on producing child after child with his lovely wife. . .'

'Stop it!' retaliated Poppy angrily. 'You're just spinning fantasies! When I said he needed me, I meant that no other secretary has ever worked so well with him. They all leave—he told me.'

'I'm not surprised! It must be like having two secretaries, the way you carry on! You're never home on time in the evenings, because Fergus *must* get this or that paper finished. You work through your lunch-hour, don't you? And when was the last time you came out with the gang in the evening?'

There was an uneasy silence while Poppy pondered on her flatmate's words. There was a strong grain of truth in all that she said. Was she in real danger of becoming a joke figure?

'Perhaps you're right,' she said unhappily. 'Perhaps the only answer is to find a different job.'

Ella leapt on to this immediately. 'When? When will you leave?'

'Not before Christmas,' Poppy replied firmly. 'The conference is in the middle of January, and I've organised the whole shebang. Whatever you might think, he does need me for that.'

'I didn't mean to be harsh,' said Ella gently. 'It's just that I can't bear to see you looking so unhappy. I only want what's best for you.'

'I know,' Poppy's voice was sad, 'I just wish there were some other way, that's all.'

Ella sat up, smiling. 'Right, that's enough serious talk for this evening. We're going to finish up these drinks, and then I'm going to concoct my world-famous stir-fried vegetables.'

'We'd better eat something,' agreed Poppy blearily. 'Even if it is your cooking—I feel half cut!' She noticed Ella's satisfied nod that she wasn't going to sit around moping for half the night. It cost her an enormous effort, but she managed to pin a wide smile to her face.

She had fallen for her boss, but Ella was perfectly

right. It would just twist the knife in further every time she saw evidence of his relationship with Catherine. And that, she was afraid, to quote Fergus, was life.

And the thought of walking out of his life made her feel particularly bleak.

She really did try. She was determined to buck up and increase her socialising. The fact that it was the run-up to Christmas helped. She and Ella had both been invited to heaps of parties, and she worked her way through each one determinedly. Night after night she stood and nodded obediently as yet another young man told her the fascinating story of his life.

Then she met a young solicitor through Ella. His name was Andrew and he was rather fun. He taught her how to play backgammon, which she loved, and took her to the theatre. She didn't know whether he was unusually perceptive, or whether Ella had said anything to him, but he seemed perfectly happy with an easy friendship. He hadn't made a single attempt to do more than kiss her lightly on the cheek.

Not that she wanted him to do anything more than that, but she had always been attractive to men. Maybe losing her heart to Fergus had destroyed all her sparkle.

Fergus had been travelling to conferences up and down the country, which made things slightly easier for her to deal with. She didn't want to see too much of his tall slimness with the characteristic slightly

loping walk. Or the quizzical humour in the light
grey eyes. Or that gorgeous way he had of brushing
the shiny brown hair from his forehead.

Oh, you simple fool, Poppy Henderson, she repri-
manded herself. Ella was right—you *are* mooning.
And if she persisted in swooning in secret about
him, then she would make it obvious to him, and
she honestly couldn't bear that.

So she tried very hard to behave normally, whatever normal might be. Catherine rang up to speak
to Fergus once and she was able to chat to her quite
politely, and even to laugh and make a small joke.

She continued to accompany Fergus on his
Wednesday ward round, and on two occasions
agreed to meet James for a drink after work.

If Fergus noticed that she had started to leave at
six, rather than at seven or eight, he made no direct
comment, but mumbled something about expecting
she had lots of shopping to do before Christmas.
The shared cups of coffee at the end of the day
seemed to have died a natural death, and their
working relationship, though functioning as satisfac-
torily as before, had become far more businesslike.

Several more women, two young, and one in late
middle age, were sent up to see Poppy by Fergus, to
demonstrate concealment make-up techniques. The
older woman was almost tearful as she thanked
Poppy for her help. She had never been able to
disguise her ugly birthmark properly until Poppy had
shown her how.

Two days later Fergus came into the office carrying a bottle of malt whisky and a box of chocolates,
and he handed her the latter.

'For you,' he smiled. 'From Mrs Brockwell.'

'The lady with the birthmark?'

'The very same. She thinks you're a miracle worker. Unless, of course,' he queried as an afterthought, 'you'd prefer the whisky? I'm not really a sexist!'

Poppy laughed. 'The chocolates will be fine—I adore truffles, and I'll probably eat the whole box!'

He couldn't help noticing the slim lushness of her young body. She didn't look as if she'd eaten a chocolate in her life. He cleared his throat hastily.

'I'm very grateful to you, Poppy,' he said in a serious voice. 'You don't have to do the make-up, but it makes such a hell of a differencce.' He glowered a little. 'It's the kind of service which should, by rights, be provided automatically, except that we don't plough enough money into hospitals any more—we just buy bombs.'

'Yes, Fergus,' she murmured. 'You can get off your soapbox now!'

He chuckled. 'You're very good for me! Don't ever leave me, will you?'

She turned to the filing cabinet. Damn and blast him! The question had been spoken half jokingly, but it had the result of making her feel terribly guilty.

She dreaded turning back to face him, afraid of what he would see written in her face, and she hated deceiving him like this—but fortunately the telephone began to ring, and Fergus picked it up.

'Yes, James?' he enquired amiably, and Poppy

knew he was speaking to his houseman. She saw Fergus's eyebrows shoot up, and a frown appear.

'Certainly,' he replied, in a markedly less amiable voice, and handed the receiver to Poppy with a look on his face she had never seen there before.

'It's James,' he announced, somewhat unnecessarily. 'For you.'

He marched over to his desk, but she knew he could hear every word. Why should he be so disapproving of James ringing her? Wasn't he even prepared to allow her a couple of minutes away from the grindstone to have a personal phone call? Miserable slavedriver!

'James—how lovely!' she said cheerily, and the bemused houseman at the other end of the phone wondered if he had got the same Poppy—she wasn't usually this affectionate.

'Lunch?' The violet eyes widened with pleasure. Just what she could do with. 'I'd love to have lunch with you. Yes, twelve-thirty's fine. I'll see you there.'

She replaced the receiver and placed some hospital headed notepaper in her typewriter, unable to miss the forbidding set of Fergus's shoulders as he sat hunched over his desk.

She began to type, acutely aware of the distinctly uneasy silence that hung in the air between them.

CHAPTER EIGHT

FERGUS was coughing for about the seventh time that morning. Poppy glanced up.

'Are you all right?' she asked.

'Of course I'm all right,' he said waspishly, blowing his nose loudly.

He didn't look all right; he looked terrible. He was pale, with a kind of glazed look in his eyes, and despite the fact that the room was already like a sauna he kept asking Poppy would she mind if he turned the heater up a little? To his annoyance, she told him she did mind. Fergus clearly had a temperature, and everyone knew you should keep the ambient temperature cool if you had a temperature. She gave a small click of disapproval with her tongue. For a doctor he could be incredibly stupid! Didn't he realise that he should be tucked up at home in bed?

But she also knew how stubborn he could be, and no amount of nagging on her part could make him go home if he had decided he was fit enough to work. She glanced once more at the light brown head bent over his papers, at the habitually crumpled shirt, and carried on with her typing.

At the next paroxysm of coughing, she could bear it no longer.

'I'm going down to the hospital shop,' she announced. 'Do you want anything?'

The grey eyes were by now even blearier. 'Do you think you could find me some throat pastilles?' he croaked.

Throat pastilles! He needed a lot more than throat pastilles, Poppy thought grimly, as she reached for her purse. Obstinate man! Why couldn't he just admit that he was ill? He had two outpatients' clincis today and he certainly shouldn't be seeing patients in that condition. Mr Khan could easily stand in for him, if only she could persuade him to go home.

She returned ten minutes later, boiled the kettle and dumped a steaming mugful of liquid on the desk in front of him.

'What's this?' he asked suspiciously.

'Well, it's not hemlock!' she snapped back, but her expression softened automatically when she saw how white his face was. 'It's Panadol and caffeine and vitamin C, made up into a lemon drink. Try it— it's quite nice.'

'Who's the doctor around here?' he grumbled.

'Shut up and drink,' she told him, not unkindly.

He didn't notice her surreptitiously turn the heating down, but she saw him pull his ancient tweed jacket closer to him.

He did actually delegate his clinics to Mr Khan, but refused to go home, and by five o'clock he was shivering, and she covered up her typewriter with a flourish.

'I'm going off now, Fergus—and so are you,' she announced.

He looked slightly dazed. 'But isn't it early. . .?'

'It's five o'clock, and you've obviously got flu. I don't want to catch it, and neither do your patients. Today's Friday, and you're not to come in until you're properly better. If you can't come in on Monday, I can arrange for Mr Khan to do your ward round and clinics for you, right?'

'Physician, heal thyself, you mean?' he asked her with a wan smile.

He rose to his feet unsteadily and she looked at him anxiously. She didn't trust him to get home safely by himself. She knew he always walked home, and that he would look at her as if she were some kind of madwoman should she have the temerity to suggest that he take a taxi.

'I'm meeting a friend up your way for an early evening drink. I'll walk with you most of the way,' she said casually.

He nodded and followed her out, letting her lock the door.

They must have made an odd-looking couple leaving the hospital, beause by now Fergus was beginning to look very ill indeed. Poppy looked round desperately for a taxi. If there was one to hand, she would just bundle him into it, argument or no argument.

Typically, there wasn't one in sight, and she didn't want to risk leaving him while she went to find one, so they began to walk.

It was a crisp, clear night which brought roses to her cheeks, but she could see Fergus's eyes glittering feverishly, as bright as the stars in the dark sky.

Concern took over from any anxiety about how
her actions might be misconstrued, and she linked
her arm with his. At least that way he was able to
lean against her as they walked along.

For Poppy it was heaven and hell mixed. Agony
and ecstasy combined. Feeling the heat of his body
next to hers as he leant against her. Feeling the
rough tweed of his jacket next to her cheek, and
being physically so close to him that she was able to
smell the wonderful scent of him, soap and tweed
and skin. She had somehow known that he would
not be the kind of man to sprinkle himself with
aftershave, and he somehow made every other man
she had ever stood close to seem like a little boy in
comparison.

She knew his address—he sometimes had his
papers typed with it at the top, instead of the
hospital letterhead. It was a long, quiet, tree-lined
road, the houses set back from a short gravel drive.
His house was number twenty-three, and Poppy was
astonished when she saw it—a serene-looking,
double-fronted Edwardian detached house, with tall
trees and shrubs surrounding it, one of which bore
bright, starry blooms. If Fergus could afford to live
in a place like this, then why on earth didn't he buy
himself some decent clothes? she wondered.

The house appeared to be in darkness, but perhaps someone was in round the back. The awful
thought had occurred to her that perhaps Catherine
lived here with him, and she didn't somehow think
she could face seeing her occupancy in evidence.

His features were indistinct in the pale light which the thin silver sliver of moon cast down upon it.

'Have you got your key with you, Fergus?' she asked softly. 'Is there anyone in? I mean—should we ring?'

He gave a start. 'Of course there's no one in—except the cat. I'll be OK now—off you go, Poppy.'

She hestitated, torn between the urge to look after him and the knowledge that she should be as far away from him as possible.

He couldn't even get the key in the lock, and she took it from him firmly and managed to get the door open. He looked at though he was in imminent danger of collapse, and she made up her mind instantly. She couldn't just abandon him.

'Can you make it upstairs?' she asked him, her arm round his waist.

'Of course I can,' he muttered, but she soon realised that he wouldn't have made it past the first stair if she hadn't been there to help him.

She half closed her eyes when they crossed the threshold of the bedroom he indicated as his own, expecting a dressing table laden with female paraphernalia, Catherine's frilly nightdress lying wispily all over the pillows, but to her surprise there was none of this, no evidence of an incumbent Catherine.

Instead there was what she might have expected if she had thought about the man who occupied it—it was total and utter chaos. It made the office on the day she had first walked into it seem like calm itself. She pushed him down on to a wicker sofa.

'Sit there and don't move,' she ordered.

The bed was in a disgusting state, with rumpled sheets and the duvet half on the floor, but at least it all looked clean. Poppy quickly remade it and plumped up the pillows; the duvet she folded neatly and placed on a chair—he was feverish and certainly didn't need its heat. She turned back to find him slumped asleep on the wicker sofa.

She shook him gently. 'Get into bed, Fergus. I'm going to fetch you something to drink.'

The kitchen defied all description, and she was sorely tempted to tackle the dishes. The only thing that stopped her was the thought that Catherine might come in in the middle of it and be slightly put out, to say the least.

She found lemon barley water and lots of ice and made up a massive jugful. She washed out a tumbler and put the whole lot on a tray, when a large fluffy ginger cat began rubbing itself against her ankles, mewing loudly. Poppy bent down and tickled its chin.

'What's up, puss?' she crooned. 'Master not fed you?'

The cat was given a large plate of food, which it began chomping on with gusto, and Poppy carried the tray upstairs.

Her cheeks flamed when she saw that Fergus had dropped all his clothes on the floor and was clearly naked beneath the thin sheet. His hair was all mussed where he'd pulled the shirt over his head, and she had to fight back the desire to smooth it down for him.

She placed the tray quietly on the locker and his eyes opened, first looking puzzled and disorientated, then he gave her an appreciative smile.

For a moment she felt the way Eve must have done before she ate the apple—the sight of this near-naked man so close to her was having the most disastrous effect on her nerves, and she had to steel herself to pour him out a glass of barley water without her hand shaking.

'You must drink two big glasses of this,' she told him. 'And then you can go to sleep. You're to take some more Panadol, but not until at least nine o'clock. And don't put that duvet back on.'

He blinked once or twice. 'How do you know so much about medicine?' he asked in a tone which she couldn't decide was admiring or sarcastic.

'It's called common sense, and I happened to do a first aid class at school,' she snapped, mainly because being crotchety seemed to be the only thing that could distract her from staring at him longingly. He had sat up to drink the barley water she handed to him, leaning down on one elbow, and the sheet had slipped to his waist. How could she have ever thought him thin? He must run, or work out, or something. You didn't get a chest like that by walking round wards or writing papers.

He flopped back against the pillow like a puppet which had had its strings cut, as if the effort of sitting up to drink had exhausted him. Poppy didn't want to leave him on his own here—but what to do?

'Is Catherine coming back tonight?' she asked, digging her nails into her hands.

The grey eyes were back to being confused. 'Catherine has her own flat,' he told her.

The heart-bursting flood of joy that this remark brought was pathetic. 'I'd better ring her up and tell her you're ill,' she said. 'What's her phone number?'

'852704,' he mumbled, and drifted off to sleep.

In the hall Poppy dialled the number he had given her, and after four or five rings a voice answered, a female voice with a faint mid-Atlantic twang, which certainly didn't sound like Catherine.

'Is Catherine there, please?' she asked.

'I'm afraid she's away,' answered the voice. 'She's at a conference in Cardiff, and we aren't expecting her back until late Sunday night.'

'Is there any way you could reach her before then?' asked Poppy desperately. 'I'm with her boyfriend, and he seems quite ill with the flu.'

'You mean Fergus?' asked the voice doubtfully.

'Yes, Fergus,' replied Poppy, a slight touch of impatience in her voice. 'Fergus Browne—I'm his secretary. He says it's viral and that there's no point seeing a doctor—he justs needs someone to keep an eye on him, that's all.'

'You mean you want Catherine to come back and *nurse* him?' The voice sounded incredulous. 'Honey, you can't know Catherine very well—the guy who's running this conference is looking for a research assistant, and Catherine wants the job real bad.'

'Look,' said Poppy calmly, 'could you at least try to get hold of her for me? Explain what's happened. If she can't come, then she might know of someone

who can. I don't know if he's got any relatives
nearby or anything—do you?'

'I've met the guy *twice*,' came the laconic reply.

'Look,' ventured Poppy, by now getting frustrated
by the phone call, 'if you like, I can try to contact
her—to save you the bother. Have you the phone
number of the conference centre?'

'No. No. She—er—I'll ring her and give her the
message. What's your name?'

'It's Henderson—Poppy Henderson.'

'OK, I'll give her the message.'

'I appreciate your help. Could you tell her that I'll
wait here for her to ring?'

'OK, I'll tell her.'

Poppy replaced the receiver, trying very hard not
to be judgemental about Catherine. If that were her,
she would be tearing down the motorway to take
care of Fergus. But she supposed that was the
difference between having a job and having a career.
Catherine couldn't just walk out of an important
conference, because she was a busy, intelligent
woman with more on her mind than the well-being
of her man. She was independent, not just an
appendage of Fergus's, and that was obviously the
kind of woman he liked. No wonder he had become
so grumpy at her own attempts to fill him up with
medicines and drinks!

Well, I don't care, she thought defiantly. The
man's ill. And people could actually die from flu.
And while no one else was around she was going to
make sure that he behaved sensibly.

She spent the next hour washing up the dishes

that had been left to accumulate in the sink, viciously applying a scouring pad to them, triumphantly seeing some of the deeper stains being removed.

But Catherine didn't ring back, and at half-past nine Poppy went back up to Fergus, to find him pale and sweating, his teeth chattering violently. She found two tablets and shook his shoulder gently.

'Wake up, Fergus,' she urged him. 'Take these— they'll make you feel better.'

Through the hazy curtain of delirium, he opened his eyes to find the lovely Poppy leaning over him like a ministering angel, putting a drink and some tablets on the locker.

'I'm cold,' he complained.

'You've got a temperature. Take those tablets quickly and drink the whole glass of barley water.'

It couldn't hurt. She was part of his dream. She wasn't real.

'I know what would make me feel better. . .' He caught her by the shoulders and, pulling her down on top of him into his arms, he began to kiss her.

For a moment she lay rigid, too shocked to move, until her lips began to be aroused by the expert way that his were moving over her mouth. For a moment she was aware of just the thin sheet separating his naked body from her, for a second her body was on fire, her mouth as aflame as his mouth.

But the heat that emanated from his body was the heat of fever, not love—not even desire, for the man was half crazed with delirium. He didn't even know who she was, let alone what he was doing.

Gently but firmly Poppy pushed him back on to

the pillow, before standing up and straightening her skirt. One thing was for sure—she couldn't stay in the same room as him, but she certainly couldn't leave him alone in the house, not in the state he was in.

'Go to sleep now,' she told him, in the voice of a mother to a sick child. 'But if you need me, call me.'

And he obeyed her instantly, like a child.

She would sleep in one of the other rooms, she thought as she went to the airing cupboard on the landing. She began to pull out single sheets, a duvet cover and a pillowcase, when suddenly an uncontrollable trembling overcame her, and she had to lean back against the wall of the small room for support.

Her cheeks burned as hotly as her mouth where Fergus had kissed her. Blood engorged her lips with a slow, steady beat that matched the relentless drumming of her heart.

He had taken her in his arms, that was all. He had an abnormally high temperature which was making him behave in a way that was completely out of character.

But he had kissed her. Crusty, brilliant, mercurial Fergus Browne had kissed her in a way she had never been kissed before.

He was the one with the fever, but Poppy felt as though she had caught the fever from him, and she had to wait until her breathing had returned to normal before she threw open the door of the spare room and began to strip the bed.

* * *

Three times she got up to him in the night—twice to give him more doses of the tablets, and once when he called out—a wild, frightened cry fuelled by his fever. She held his hand tightly until his breathing was easier, then fetched a cloth dampened in very cold water, dabbing away at his forehead and his temples until she was satisfied that he was cooler as he slept.

In the morning he didn't seem much better; his temperature was still high, and he stared at her with unfocused eyes. Poppy made up her mind instantly—she would telephone the doctor, whether Fergus liked it or not.

By the telephone in the hall she found a black address book and skimmed through it until she had found the address of his general practitioner.

She was informed by a receptionist that Dr Wells would be able to call and visit at around midday, after he had done his Saturday morning emergency clinic. Poppy glanced at her watch—it was now nine-fifteen and there was plenty of time to tidy up a bit before he came. She had a wash and eyed her clothes dubiously. Apart from the fact that they were her work clothes, and not very suitable for heavy-duty housework, they were already very crumpled and tired-looking. She hunted around and eventually found a black track-suit which must have been Fergus's, judging by the length of the arms and legs. It was very baggy on her, but with a little rolling up and tucking in she had soon produced a perfectly functional working garment.

She made herself a cup of black coffee—the milk

looked as though it ought to have a government
health warning on it—which she drank before deciding where to start first. The kitchen, definitely.
Looking round her, she was surprised that Fergus
hadn't come down with typhoid long ago!

She found cloths, a mop, dustpan and brush,
various bottles of cleaning agents, and set to work
with a vengeance. It was enormously satisfying to
see the change that her efforts had wrought. It was
exactly like one of the 'before' and 'after' shots that
advertisers were so keen on showing on television.
She washed up everything that she could lay her
hands on swept and cleaned out cupboards and put
their contents away tidily, and finally she scrubbed
the floor twice before she was satisfied with the
result.

Next she set to work on the rest of the downstairs.
She took one look at Fergus's study and decided it
was best left alone. Instead she tidied, dusted and
Hoovered the hall and the sitting-room, dumping a
long-dead pot-plant unceremoniously in the bin. The
man had his head in the clouds, without a doubt! He
could write papers and books that had made his
name famous all over the world—and yet he lived in
the most shabby surroundings she had even seen.
No wonder he dressed like a scruffy student—seeing
the state of his house, Poppy was only surprised that
he managed to find any clean clothes at all!

He needed someone to look after him, and
Catherine was evidently useless at the job, she
thought before amending the thought swiftly. He
needed a housekeeper—someone who could keep

the house tidy, as he was obviously one of those men who didn't expect his girlfriend to be a dogsbody around the house.

But he needed more than that, she thought wistfully. The house was crying out for some love and attention. It was a perfect house—high ceilings, exquisite mouldings and a grand and impressive fireplace in the sitting-room. It needed coals burning red and warm in the grate, fresh flowers on the tables, embroidered cushions on the faded but splendid old sofa—and wallpaper and paint lavished upon it.

You really do need your head examined, Poppy thought as she sang tunelessly and happily, flicking a large cobweb from the side of a table lamp.

By eleven-thirty she had the downstairs gleaming, and ran upstairs two at a time to take a look at Fergus and tidy up his room in preparation for the doctor while she was about it.

He was sound asleep, with stubble on his chin from where he had not shaved. She allowed herself one longing look—the stubble made him look as handsome as any actor, she thought, her eyes transfixed by the sight of one very lean shoulder and arm. She picked up his clothes from the floor and folded them into a pile, reddening a little at the intimacy of this action, and, hearing the doorbell, made her way downstairs. Perhaps she should have straightened the sheet, but after what had happened last night. . . She blushed once more and opened the door.

Tom Wells, the GP, eyed the tall girl in black with the shiny hair and the pink cheeks with interest.

And just who was she? He thought Fergus had a long-standing relationship with the dark-haired doctor—what was her name now?—Catherine, that was it. He and his wife had met them at a party ages ago. So who was this beautiful young creature with the amazing eyes?

'Hello,' he said, smiling pleasantly. 'I'm Tom Wells, Fergus's GP. Who are you?'

You couldn't help warming to a man who had a pen shaped like a plastic carrot sticking out of the top pocket of his tweed coat. He saw her looking at it, and smiled again.

'It makes the children laugh,' he explained. 'Makes them less scared of the doctor.'

It made Poppy want to laugh too. 'I'm Poppy Henderson—I work as Fergus's secretary. I'm afraid he's ill—he seems to have a bad fever. I wasn't sure if I was doing the right things, and he still looks a bit poorly this morning. I do hope I haven't called you out unnecessarily. . .'

'No, no, no.' He held his hand up, stopping her in mid-flow. 'You look a sensible enough lassie to me. Now take your time, and tell me what's wrong with the old devil.'

Poppy told him as clearly as she could. 'I've been giving him Panadol every four hours,' she said.

'And is he drinking?'

'Quite well. He needs a bit of forcing, but I've managed to get two jugfuls of barley water inside him.'

He looked pleasantly surprised. 'You're not a nurse, are you?'

'Good heavens, no! I have four younger brothers, that's all.'

Fergus woke up a bit when Dr Wells shook him gently awake.

'Ouch!' he croaked. 'My throat hurts!'

'Then stop talking,' said the GP, pulling out his stethoscope.

'What are you doing here, Tom?'

'Trying to examine you. Now open wide and say "ahh!"'

'Ahh!'

Poppy smiled and left the room, and was downstairs in the kitchen when Tom Wells came back in.

'Would you like a cup of coffee, Doctor?' she asked. 'There's no milk, I'm afraid.'

'I can imagine,' he responded drily. 'I won't stop, thank you, m'dear. You're doing excellently—and more of the same is what I'd prescribe. He won't want to eat much, but you might try him with a little soup later.' His curiosity got the better of him. 'Er—it's very good of you to give up your weekend like this. Catherine isn't around, then?'

If Dr Wells had hit her very hard over the head with a frying pan, he couldn't have upset her more. But of course he would ask. He probably knew Catherine.

'Oh, Catherine's away at a conference in Wales,' she told him airily. 'I'm trying to get hold of her—she's supposed to be ringing me back.'

'Ah, yes, of course. Ever the career girl, the lovely Catherine.'

Which she, Poppy, wasn't. And never would be.

Tom Wells bent to fasten his Gladstone bag. So that was the way the wind lay. He'd thought as much when he'd seen her standing at his bedside. There was a way a woman had of looking at a man she was in love with when she thought she was unobserved, and Poppy had been gazing at the dermatologist with a tenderness that went beyond the realms of a working relationship. The man must be mad, he thought. Catherine might be an intellectual heavyweight, but he had thought her a cold woman. This young creature looked as if she would care for Fergus in a way that Catherine never had.

He said as much to his wife that evening. 'The man's a fool if he can't see what's staring him in the face,' he opined, as he threw another log on to the fire.

'Why, Tom,' said his wife reprovingly, 'if I didn't know you better, I'd say that this secretary of Fergus Browne's had stolen your heart away!'

The GP laid his glass of whisky on the side table. 'She's no lovelier than you were when I first met you twenty-five years ago,' he said gruffly. 'No lovelier than you look tonight.'

'Oh, darling!' She gazed at him fondly.

Poppy waited in until four o'clock, but Catherine had still not rung, and she badly needed to stock up with provisions. She would just have to risk being out if the call came. She let herself out of the back door and took a brisk walk to the grocery store at the end of Fergus's road. She bought milk, bread, butter, eggs, soup, chocolate, cheeses, fruit and a newspaper. When she returned to the house it was in darkness, and she had just checked on Fergus, who was still asleep, but a much better colour, and was putting the kettle on to make herself a cup of tea, when the telephone rang.

It was Catherine, and she was brief and to the point.

'Hi. What's the problem?'

Poppy had half expected her to be indignant, jealous even—that her position was being usurped, albeit temporarily. She hadn't expected this clear, almost indifferent question.

'Fergus is ill,' she explained. 'The doctor's been in—and he doesn't really think he should be left alone.'

'Oh?' The cool voice sounded faintly amused. 'But he's not, is he? Alone, I mean. After all, you're there.'

Poppy couldn't believe what she was hearing. Didn't Catherine mind that she was there? Didn't she care that Fergus was ill?

'Unless,' a note of doubt had entered the smooth voice, 'unless you've something planned, and can't stay there?'

'Well, no, as a matter of fact, I haven't,' Poppy told her.

'I thought not. Well then, problem solved. You can stay with him can't you?'

Poppy was taken aback, to say the least—there was nothing like being taken for granted, but perhaps Catherine suspected as much, since she hastily amended her previous statement with a far more conciliatory tone.

'Listen, Poppy,' she said, using her Christian name for the first time, 'I'm after a job, and I think I'm going to get it—I just may have to hang around a bit, that's all.'

'Why, when does the conference finish?'

Now Catherine sounded impatient. 'It finished last night—but you don't understand. A job of the status I'm going for needs—well, let's just say that I have to make sure that I get on with the rest of the team.' There was a muffled voice in the background. 'Listen—I have to go. Tell Fergus I'll try to call him tomorrow. OK, Poppy? Bye, then.'

Poppy hung up and walked slowly back to the kitchen to finish making her tea. She toasted a currant bun and buttered it, then took the tray into the sitting-room, where she sipped and munched thoughtfully.

How strange to live your life as Fergus and Catherine obviously did. Two attractive and intelligent people who had a long-standing and obviously mutually satisfying relationship, yet their worlds seemed hardly to touch. And where was Catherine's new job going to take her?

Poppy had grown up in a wild, warm family of five children with never quite enough of anything to go round, not quite enough meat, or clothes or new shoes. But Mama had told them to fill up on bread and jam, and old shoes could be cleaned and passed down—and to make up for all that there had been the sense of caring, of belonging. The warm bosom

of a family. Something she'd always thought she
might emulate. Perhaps that was why she had no
interest in the Julians of this world, with their flashy
cars and their jobs in advertising. She couldn't see
Julian tramping through misty woods in order that
they might find logs to build the fire—the fire on
which they would roast their sweet chestnuts and
toast the bread to eat with the sticky home-made
jam. Nor James either, really.

And wasn't that something of what attracted her
to Fergus? With his determined lack of city sophisti-
cation, he *was* a man she could see in that role.
More was the pity that he didn't know anything
about it!

After her tea and bun she had a long bath,
changed back into another old tracksuit, and
bundled a heap of clothes into his ancient washing
machine.

At seven she went in to find him sitting up, staring
at her with an expression that could only be
described as incredulous.

Fergus blinked again. Poppy? In his bedroom?
What on earth. . .?

She was so relieved to see him looking more like
his normal self that any embarrassment or constraint
she might otherwise have felt was instantly forgotten, and she beamed at him, a smile so wide it
almost split her face in two.

'Thank goodness you're better!' she exclaimed,
and then, seeing the still puzzled look in his eyes,
she went on to explain. 'You've been ill, Fergus—
don't you remember? Your temperature was up in

the sky, and you were talking a load of gibberish.'
And you kissed me—don't you remember?

Fergus frowned. His head was splitting and his
mouth felt as if someone had lit a fire in it, leaving
him with only the burnt-out remains. Yet there was
a memory that eluded him. Dimly, through distant
hazes of the last twenty-four hours, small instants
came back to him. Feeling lousy at the hospital.
Poppy bossing him about. Walking home on a cold,
frosty night with her. And then?

And Poppy seemed to be staring at him with a
slight air of unease, as if she too were waiting for
him to remember something.

'I can't remember anything,' he admitted.

She gave a high laugh. 'There isn't very much to
remember, I gave you painkillers every four hours,
forced you to drink your barley water. . .'

'Yeuk!' he joked weakly.

'I called in your doctor too.'

'Tom Wells?' He sounded surprised. 'You didn't
have to do that.'

He caught a sudden glimpse of uncertainty in
those beautiful violet eyes of hers.

'I wasn't sure myself whether to call him. I knew
you might be cross! But he was very sweet. He said
you could have some soup if you wanted it.' Poppy's
voice was shy. Dealing with a recovering non-deliri-
ous Fergus in the bizarre and intimate environment
of his bedroom was making her feel less self-assured
by the moment. 'Are you hungry?'

He grinned. 'Now you're talking—I'm starving! I

can see I'm going to have to pay you overtime for all this special treatment!'

The cloud of happiness which had been enveloping her in all its comforting warmth suddenly evaporated. Now she felt out of place. *De trop*. What was she, an employee, doing in her boss's bedroom?

She moved awkwardly to the door. 'I'll make you something. Then I'm afraid I'll have to go.'

When she returned she saw that he'd washed, remade the bed and donned a pyjama jacket which looked so new that she guessed he hardly ever wore it. And seeing him in it seemed to bring to the forefront of her mind his nakedness over the past day. The stubble had been removed too, and the hair brushed. It was time she left.

He eyed the bowl of tomato soup, the neat soldiers of toast and the tea in the pristinely clean china cup and saucer. 'This looks wonderful!' he smiled.

'I don't think you need me any more, do you?' said Poppy. 'This is my phone number in case you do. Catherine says she'll try to ring on her way back from Wales tomorrow.'

He nodded absently, staring at he intently, trying to work out what he had said that was wrong. What had caused that cold little look on her face that he'd never seen there before?

'You're a girl in a million,' he said, immediately wanting to kick himself for the trite-sounding line. He damn well meant it, so why did it have to come out like the corny come-on of some has-been Hollywood star?

The soft lips curved into a dutiful smile, and again some warning bell rang deep in his subconscious.

'I'll see you on Monday,' Poppy said formally. 'I hope you're feeling better.' Her hand on the door, she turned round suddenly. 'Oh, Fergus?'

He just wanted her to relax, to see the smile he had grown to know so well. He looked at her hopefully. 'Poppy?'

'I've fed the cat.'

At any other time, the absurdity of this flat statement would have made them both look at each other and break into peals of laughter, but not this time.

He could hear her moving down the stairs, shutting the front door behind her.

Outside, the stars were already beginning to sprinkle the sky and she took a deep breath.

It was as she suspected, as common sense had told her it would be—he had been delirious when he had kissed her. He had kissed her like a man who had wanted to make love. To be kissed like that by the man she had grown to love had been like the fulfilment of her wildest dreams.

He had kissed her and he had forgotten that he had ever done so, and things were never going to be the same again.

CHAPTER NINE

LITTLE was said about Fergus's illness. When Poppy returned to work on the Monday, it was as if it had never happened—he looked and behaved as normal. Except that there was a new, hidden tension in the air which had the effect of making them much more polite with each other than they had been before. He had thanked her gruffly for all she had done, but was clearly embarrassed at having had her nurse him in his own home, and Poppy just wanted to forget about the whole thing.

And the department was incredibly busy in the run-up to Christmas, as Fergus remarked one morning when he saw the extended list for his outpatient clinic.

In the past she would have asked the question eagerly; now it came out listlessly. 'Why should it be so busy?'

Fergus looked up from the letters he was signing. 'Because a lot of skin conditions are stress-induced, and Christmas is a very stressful time, isn't it?'

'Christmas!' Poppy exclaimed disbelievingly. 'Stressful?' It certainly hadn't been stressful at home—all of them spending weeks making their small presents and saving up their money to buy what they could from Riley's on the corner. They would glue together paper chains and hang them in gaudy festoons all over the draughty old house. And the goose would be brought over from the Donovans' farm, killed that Christmas Eve morning for cooking the next day, and for many years Poppy would eat only vegetables—she felt so sorry for the goose! And they would open their presents and drink a glass of port, and after the big roast dinner her father would get out the old fiddle and they'd all sing along. . .no, it certainly hadn't been stressful at home.

Fergus was sitting very still, looking at her. 'You looked miles away,' he said gently.

'So I was,' she said briskly, and then, because she couldn't cope with his being gentle, she fired a question at him. 'And why do you say it's stressful?'

His eyes looked a bit sad. 'Because people's expectations are too high, that's why. They get bombarded with images from the media, the big hype of everyone sitting round the tree, laughing with delight as they open their presents, a big circle of family unity.'

'And what's wrong with that?' she asked indignantly.

'Because it's often nothing like that,' he returned. 'People get bogged down by the material side of Christmas, and by the time it comes they're too tired to enjoy themselves. Then Granny puts her foot in it, they've all had too much to drink, and the next thing you know, they're all falling out.'

'Maybe in England they do,' said Poppy, and he laughed.

'Why, Poppy, what a very partisan thing to say! Do I take it you're off home for Christmas?'

'I'm not sure yet,' she mumbled, and put some fresh paper in her typewriter with an air of finality which suggested that the subject was no longer for discussion. Damn him, she thought. They weren't supposed to be *having* these kind of personal chats, hadn't that been his rule—told to her on the very day she arrived? She could remember it word for word even now—'someone who will not attempt to engage me in what I believe is popularly known as "chit-chat".' She supposed he had mellowed since that day, but she didn't want him to mellow. She wouldn't be going all weak at the knees and foolish if he were still behaving like the arrogant despot she'd met on her first day.

And she wasn't sure at all whether she wanted to go home, not this year. For one thing, it would be tight getting the fare together. But the main reason was that she didn't want to spoil their holiday—not when she was feeling so miserable herself. And her mother would know that something was up. There would be questions asked, and opinions offered— perhaps she ought not be working for a man she might be in danger of making a fool of herself over. Her mother might think she was in danger of being 'taken advantage of'. One of her brothers might even be sent over for a 'holiday'. Heaven forbid! thought Poppy, and shuddered. Why not simply save all the trouble and take up Ella's invitation to go and stay with her family? Next Christmas she wouldn't even know a Fergus Browne to mention.

Ella had nagged her to death on Sunday night when she had arrived home from her Mission of Mercy at Fergus's, as it had been sarcastically called, and Poppy had told her that her definite date for leaving would be during the last week in January, when the conference would be over.

That week on the ward round, she couldn't help noticing how busy the ward looked. All the beds were full, and Fergus was unusually bad-tempered when he asked Geoff, the charge nurse, about the bed state.

'I've got four patients who *must* come in, Geoff.'

The tall, bearded charge nurse raised his shoulders, his eyes and his hands to heaven.

'What can I do, Fergus?' he pleaded. 'I've got three who by rights are medically fit to go home, yet socially they aren't equipped to do so. Two old ladies who should be in ground floor flats, both in high-rise blocks where the lift is vandalised frequently.

'I've one old boy who just can't cope on his own, his daughter won't take him, and he's refusing to go into the local home, because the stories circulating about it locally are so horrendous that all the pensioners think it's run by the Marquis de Sade. So what's your solution?'

'Pah!' exploded Fergus, so loudly that a physiotherapist assisting a lady on a zimmer frame looked up in alarm. 'I'll tell you what the solution is!' he raged, not caring who heard him. 'The whole lot of us right now should walk out of here to Downing Street and present a bloody great petition to the government, telling them to spend less money on their bloody missiles, and a bit more on people's health. That's *my* solution!'

As he strode ahead of the trolley she saw the group lift their eyes heavenwards, as if to say, here we go again! But Poppy was not one of them. It was one of the sides of Fergus she admired most—the caring, charismatic doctor, vociferously voicing his commitment to the Health Service. Whether or not you liked the man, you could not help admiring him.

In between patients, Fergus's face stayed set with anger, but when he examined the ill people on his ward, he did it with a gentleness and a thoroughness that took your breath away. The last patient was situated in one of the two small side-cubicles nearest the office. These single rooms usually housed patients who needed a lot of nursing attention, or those who had an infectious disease, or who were very sick.

The little old lady who lay in there obviously came under the category of the very sick. The team spoke in hushed voices, so as not to disturb her. Poppy had never seen Fergus quite so tender as when he examined her, even helping Geoff to rearrange her pillows afterwards, his face grave.

Afterwards, she saw him standing apart from the others in the office, gazing unseeingly at the calendar on the wall, his cup of coffee untouched, the delicious chocolate cake untasted. She couldn't help herself—sometimes where Fergus was concerned some instinctual feeling took over, and she went up and gently touched his elbow.

'Are you thinking about that patient?' she asked quietly.

The grey eyes swivelled to stare at her very hard for a moment. Fergus sometimes felt defensive about the way he felt, he knew that a good doctor should not care too deeply, but on some occasions you just couldn't *not* care. He saw the expression on Poppy's face and his own softened into a smile.

'Yes, I suppose I am.'

'She's very ill, isn't she?'

Now his reply was very gentle. He sometimes forgot just how young she was—how little she really knew. 'She's dying, Poppy.'

Her violet eyes were troubled. 'But she's all on her own—no one should have to die on their own.'

How simple the world was when you were that age, he thought. Everything was black and white— few shadings of grey. 'You're not in Ireland now, you know,' he said gently.

'And more's the pity,' she returned. 'Because no one would leave an old lady on her own like that. Hasn't she any family?'

'She has a daughter—a most delightful woman. She's married "up" is, I believe, the term. Her husband works in the City and earns a great deal of money, and their two daughters attend exclusive schools. They live in an enormous house that sits in the middle of eight acres of prime Sussex land, where the mother could have very easily been accommodated. But they can't have Mrs Hanrahan living with them—no, indeed. Mrs Hanrahan is an embarrassment to her daughter and son-in-law, and to their friends. She doesn't know which knife she should pick up. She likes to drink tea from a mug, and she eats leftovers for her supper because she can't bear to see waste.'

She had never heard him this sarcastic before, or seen the bitter, angry look on his face. Her face grew shocked as he recounted the treatment meted out to the old woman.

'But surely the daughter's coming to visit her mother now?' she stammered. 'She has been coming to see her?'

His mouth tightened. 'They're holidaying in the Bahamas—the husband desperately "needs" the break, and it's been arranged for so long that they couldn't possibly cancel it now.'

Poppy stared at him for a moment longer. What a strange world it was! What a rotten world, where people could just shrug off family ties, could disregard a mother as though she were of no consequence.

That evening Fergus went to the ward late, to find James West hanging around in the office, looking slightly ill at ease.

'Hello, James,' he said in some surprise. 'You're here very late, aren't you? We're not on call tonight.'

'Er—no.' He had actually gone a little pink around the ears, Fergus noted. 'I'm just hoping I might be able to persuade Poppy to come out for a drink with me.'

Fergus made a huge effort to quell the irrational flash of anger that shot through him at the thought

of his handsome young houseman luring his secretary off to a pub somewhere. 'Poppy?' he asked in
surprise. 'Well, you won't find her here. She went
home hours ago.'

'She didn't, you know.'

Fergus was irritated now. 'Oh, for goodness' sake,
man, will you stop talking in riddles? Where is
Poppy?'

'She's sitting with the old lady in cubicle two,'
explained James, his face still pink. 'She doesn't
want her to be on her own.'

Fergus nodded, and walked quietly out into the
corridor. It was very still, and large decorations in
shiny metallic colours hung above the oxygen cylin-
ders, the wheelchairs and all the other functional
paraphernalia of hospital life. He walked until he
reached the cubicle and stood by the half-open door
for a moment, watching her.

She sat on a hard chair beside the bed, leaning
forward, holding the bony, gnarled old hand in both
her own, and her lips were moving slightly. Fergus
thought she was probably praying. For a moment he
wanted to go in there and be with her. To share her
sweet, lonely vigil with her. To stand behind her
chair with his strong hands holding those slim
shoulders, protecting her, supporting her.

He shook his head. He must not intrude. He
continued to walk down the ward towards the
patient he wanted to examine. When he came back
he saw that Poppy had not moved. Except that she
was no longer alone. Now there were two nurses in
there as well, and they were wheeling a trolley. And

as he made to move, one of the nurses walked up to the door, her face grave, and closed the small wooden shutter.

Fergus found James still waiting in the office.

'Listen, James—why don't you get off home now? I can always see that Poppy gets home safely, and besides, there's an urgent letter she's promised to type for me.' The lie came out as smoothly as though he uttered one every sentence.

For a moment James regarded his boss guardedly. Surely he wasn't after Poppy? No, definitely not. Not someone like Fergus, and certainly *not* someone as bubbly as Poppy!

'Sure,' he said easily. 'I'll see you tomorrow. Thanks, Fergus.' As he walked down the main corridor he began to wonder just who it should have been thanking whom.

Fergus stood staring out of the window when he heard the door open. He turned round to see Poppy looking distraught, the wide violet eyes brimming with tears.

'Oh, Fergus.' Her voice broke on a sob. 'She's. . .she's. . .'

He didn't say a word, just held his arms open wide, and she ran into them, sobbing great noisy sobs against his jacket.

'I know, Poppy,' he whispered. 'It's all right—I know.'

He didn't know how long they stood there for, or who saw them, and he didn't care. He could have gone on holding her all night.

And later, when he'd put her into a taxi, he stood

for ages in the cold, and it occurred to him that he had little to go home to, or for. An empty, cold house as usual.

There was something very unsettling about Poppy, he thought. She seemed to epitomise something that he was yearning for. He had started to feel lonely in the evenings—an academic life was OK, but it had its limitations. His long-standing relationship with Catherine had always suited them both perfectly well—so why was he beginning to feel that it was not enough? Catherine was passionately committed to her career, she must go where the best jobs were—they had always agreed on that. An ideal compromise for a modern romance. Or was it?

He realised that he hadn't seen her for weeks and weeks. What on earth was happening to them?

As he turned his head to the chill wind, he couldn't remember ever having felt so utterly confused.

CHAPTER TEN

'FERGUS is having a party,' announced Poppy, sitting back on her heels and clearing a little space for herself among the piles of brightly coloured wrapping paper.

Ella drew a sprig of holly on one of the gift tags, then frowned. 'A party, you say? A great Christmas rave-up, you mean? I must say he doesn't really sound the type.'

'He isn't,' Poppy sighed. 'It's a drinks party at his house.' There was a long pause. 'He's having it with Catherine.'

Ella stopped wrapping a red plastic fire engine for her nephew. She had never met Fergus Browne, yet she disliked him intensely. Ever since the first day that Poppy had gone to work for him, their lives had been made a misery. Even now, when Poppy was so obviously trying to be 'civilised' about the fact that he was holding a party with his long-standing girlfriend, Ella could sense her friend's underlying disquiet. She knew Poppy so well, and she hated to see her like this—the dark shadows under her eyes, the face which had grown pale, and whose high cheekbones were now even more defined, because she had lost pounds since working for the wretched Fergus.

She saw Poppy gazing at her expectantly, and sighed to herself. She would be the good friend. She

126

could see that Poppy was keen to talk, so she would let her gabble away, although she could already guess what line the conversation would take—the line all conversations took these days—they all led back to this dermatologist who sounded as though he kitted himself out at the local Oxfam shop!

'So—are you going?' she asked.

'I honestly don't know.' Poppy's expression was serious as she idly twiddled with a piece of metallic sticky tape. How could she begin to explain to Ella that, while she dreaded the thought of seeing him there, entwined with Catherine, some perverse masochistic urge was dragging her on; she *wanted* to go, and she couldn't understand why. 'Would you think I was mad if I did go?'

'Of course I wouldn't. It's natural you'd want to go—you think you love him, therefore you want to see him as much as possible. Your imagination is working overtime—you think Catherine won't be there, and that he'll grab you into his arms and tell you you're the only woman for him. Don't you?'

Poppy assumed a lofty look. 'Don't be so daft!' she sniffed.

'Liar!'

She decided to abandon this particular topic. 'Do you think I should go, then?'

There was a rustle of paper. 'I think perhaps you should—maybe if you see them canoodling round the floor together, it might finally make you see sense, although I doubt it. Can't you take anyone?'

'That's what *he* suggested,' said Poppy gloomily, remembering how her boss's polite invitation that she might want to bring a partner had caused her to be miserable all afternoon. 'James has said he'll take me.'

'Well, there you are, then!' Ella most definitely did approve of James, and thought Poppy needed her head examining if she let him go without a struggle. With those crisp blond curls and that amazing physique—*she* certainly wouldn't turn him down! And he was obviously bananas about Poppy, if she would only forget about Dr Skin.

After lengthy and earnest debate, it was decided that Poppy *would* go, and that James would accompany her. She then drove Ella nearly to distraction by her mood swings. One moment she was going to treat it as just any old party and wear the cleanest thing in her wardrobe, the next she would be scouring exclusive boutiques for something perfect which they both knew that she couldn't afford without causing her bank manager to have apoplexy.

In the end, and much against her better judgement, Ella allowed Poppy to persude her to lend her one very good dress which had cost a king's ransom in last year's January sales. It was black and short and very cleverly cut—there appeared to be yards of material in the skirt, and yet above that it clung to every curve.

The night before Christmas Eve found Poppy teetering along the icy pavements in unusually high heels, clutching on to James for support. He had been delighted to accompany her to the party. She had told him, quite plainly, that while she liked him

very much indeed she was not at all interested in
pursuing his proposed romantic entanglement.

That was fine, he had told her—and he would still
be more than delighted to accompany her to the
party. James was one of those undeniably handsome
men who were so used to females falling over
backwards to go out with him that he was irresistibly
drawn to the one woman who seemed totally
immune to his charms. However, such was his
healthy young ego that he envisaged no problem in
eventually wearing down her defences.

As they approached the elegant house, Poppy
remembered the last time she'd been here—when
Fergus had been so ill. She wondered how Catherine
had really felt about that. But she need have no
cause to worry—it had all been perfectly innocent.
Then she remembered the ardent and feverish kiss,
and shivered a little in the darkness as James rang
the doorbell. It wasn't *her* fault, she thought
crossly—she had tried to get Catherine to come and
nurse him, but she had refused. And the poor man
couldn't have been left alone like that.

Inside the large Edwardian house—which was
looking unaccustomedly bright and festive with the
great sprigs of mistletoe and holly which Catherine
had been standing on step-ladders and erecting all
afternoon—Fergus again felt utterly confused.

It had been Catherine's suggestion that they have
the party, and he absolutely hated parties, but she
had been so determined. So determined, in fact, that
he had wondered whether she was choosing this
particular moment to announce to the world that

they were about to become engaged. For some
reason, he had gone hot and cold at this. It wasn't
that he had anything against marriage, or indeed
against marriage to Catherine—they had both kind
of assumed that one day they would. But the time
had never been right, in fact it wasn't right just
now—Catherine was working miles away, and there
would be another four years at least before she got
her consultancy and could think of settling down.

But fortunately, no engagements were discussed.
In fact they discussed very little—Catherine seemed
so busy with all the party arrangements. The other
night he had realised that, apart from that one brief
lunch, it was getting on for almost three months
since they had seen one another, and even the phone
calls had been sparse of late. So, what with one thing
and another, he was psyching himself up for a
romantic weekend with her.

Except that things had not quite transpired that
way. Firstly, she had not arrived late on the Friday
evening, as promised. She had appeared on the
Saturday morning with a grinning fair man who was
introduced as Philip.

'He's my boss,' she had smiled, and Fergus had
blinked slightly as they had shaken hands.

Her boss? It seemed a rather peculiar thing to
bring your boss all the way from Wales for a drinks
party. And it seemed that her boss had certain
sensibilities. Apparently it was going to be inadvis-
able for her and Fergus to share a room together as
Philip would be staying the night of the party.

'He won't like it,' Catherine had hissed.

Quite what right her consultant had to concern himself in Catherine's sex life, Fergus couldn't imagine, but, disturbingly, he felt rather relieved about the whole thing and raised no objections whatsoever. After the conference he really *ought* to have a holiday, he decided as he put some more champagne in the fridge to chill.

He watched with a rather bemused expression as Philip regaled a group of people in the corner, Catherine amongst them, with a story Fergus had already heard that day, about the nursing officer who had locked the Chief of Surgery in the operating theatre by mistake. It wasn't a particularly riveting story, he thought—yet Catherine stood gazing up at him as if she were at the feet of the prophet. Extraordinary.

Then the doorbell rang, and Fergus opened it, almost dropping his glass of champagne when he saw Poppy and James standing there. He had been sure she wouldn't come—she had been so huffy when he had invited her. He forced himself to shake hands with his houseman as he ushered them inside, but felt strangely tongue-tied as he helped Poppy out of her coat. He felt a ridiculous urge to run his hands down her back, to encircle her waist. Surely that body couldn't be for real? She looked. . .she looked. . .utterly dynamic. Utterly. He hastily put his half-finished glass of champagne down on the hall table as he went to hang up their coats and fetch them a drink.

The party passed in a blur for Poppy. She was aware that there were a lot of people milling around, laughing and chatting—indeed, she and James were introduced to many of them, and she went through the motions of enjoying conversations with a diverse selection of guests.

But she was aware too of Catherine's presence—as graceful as a butterfly in a floaty dress of palest pink, which set off the dark, glossy wings of her raven hair to perfection. She steeled herself to watch as Catherine laid a proprietorial hand on Fergus's arm from time to time, or stopped for a fleeting kiss when she thought that they were unobserved, but to her surprise there were no open displays of affection. Perhaps that was the correct way to do things—after all, they weren't teenagers.

Catherine seemed to spend most of her time chatting to a brawny-looking man with shiny fair hair who was introduced as Philip, her boss.

By ten o'clock, Poppy knew that she'd had enough and looked around for James, but he was nowhere to be seen. Perhaps he was in the kitchen, or the study. Easily the tallest girl in the room, she moved towards the door.

Fergus saw her go and, smiling charmingly, excused himself from the company of his elderly next-door neighbour.

Away from the hubbub of the party, the large hall was strangely silent, save for the melodic ticking of the large grandfather clock that stood in one of the recesses, and she was reminded of how it chimed so beautifully on the hour.

There was a slight noise behind her and she turned round, her bright smile becoming a mask when she saw who it was. She was so afraid he would guess how she really felt about him that she was determined he should read nothing of it in her face.

She had never seen him dressed up before, and he looked wonderful. He wore black, tapered trousers which emphasised the lean, muscular length of his legs, the narrow hips. And a shirt of a white silky material, open at the neck—which served to make him look nothing like the brilliant consultant she worked for, but more like some ancient buccaneer. She realised she was having difficulty controlling her breathing, and she blurted out the first thing which came into her head.

'I—I was just looking for James,' she stammered. 'We really ought to be making tracks.'

'Oh? Must you?' She thought he looked disappointed.

He found himself staring down into the luminous violet eyes, at the full lips which seemed so tremulous tonight. He suddenly had a mad urge to kiss her. He cleared his throat and lifted a wrapped parcel from the bureau next to the grandfather clock.

'This is for you,' he said, handing it to her.

Poppy was actually afraid she was going to drop it. 'Oh, you shouldn't have,' she replied automatically, wishing someone would come, that James would appear to break this strange atmosphere that had descended on them.

'Oh, yes, I should.' The grey eyes were terribly serious. 'I haven't even really thanked you properly for the way you looked after me when I was ill. . .'

'It—it was nothing,' she said, wishing that he would let her go before she did or said something irrevocably foolish.

'It was,' Fergus said firmly. 'I'm sure that playing nursemaid to me isn't part of your contract.' He smiled as if trying to lighten the atmosphere. 'But nothing about your work would surprise me—you've been the best secretary I've ever had, and having you there to support me makes all the difference to my work.'

Poppy bit her lip. And I'm going to leave you after the conference, Fergus. I wonder what you'll think of me then.

'You're not to open that until Christmas Day,' he smiled. 'Isn't that what your mother always told you?'

'Yes, she did.'

He frowned, puzzled by her unusual lack of verbal response. 'You're not going home for Christmas, I take it?'

'No—there's not really time. I'm going to stay with my flatmate's parents in the country.'

He nodded, wishing there was something he could do to bring back the old Poppy.

Just then something fell from the ceiling, dropping on to the wooden floor and bouncing off it with an unnaturally loud ping. It was a small white berry. At exactly the same time, they looked up to see the sprig of mistletoe that hung almost directly over their heads. The silence became deafening, and Fergus was unable to stop himself.

'Happy Christmas, Poppy,' he said softly, and kissed her.

It was not a long kiss and it was certainly not an intimate kiss—compared to the heady passion of his feverish kiss, it was about as chaste as the kiss of one playmate for another. But it affected them both profoundly.

They both stepped back, each staring at the other, as if seeking the answer to some question which neither dared ask.

Poppy often wondered what would have happened had James not appeared, with Catherine following.

'So here you are!' he exclaimed cheerily, then glancing from one to the other, he frowned. 'There's nothing wrong, is there, Poppy?'

Poppy forced herself to answer, in a voice she didn't quite recognise as her own. 'Of course not. I was just saying goodnight to Fergus.' She turned to Catherine. 'It's been nice seeing you again,' she managed to say, feeling the worst kind of hypocrite as she did so. 'Merry Christmas.'

'And to you,' echoed Catherine. 'Aren't you going to fetch their coats?' she asked Fergus, fixing him with a very long look.

'Yes, of course.'

There was a flurry of farewells and some late arrivals, so that Poppy was able to leave the house without having to meet Fergus's eyes again. She was very quiet as they walked along the pavement, which had grown steadily frostier even while they had been at the party.

'Who's that parcel for?' enquired James with interest.

'For me,' she said quietly.

'Oh?'

'It's from Fergus,' she explained reluctantly.

'From Fergus? That's a turn-up for the books! Aren't you going to open it?'

'No, I'm not,' she said firmly, tucking it under her arm. 'He doesn't want me to—not until Christmas morning.'

'Oh, come *on*, Poppy—that's just for kids!'

She shook her head, knowing she would not go out with James again after tonight. He deserved something better than a girl who had hopelessly lost her heart to someone else.

On Christmas morning, she left Fergus's present until last, wanting to cherish the thought that he had bought something especially for her, had sat and wrapped it.

She knew that Ella was watching her as she carefully slit open the paper and took out something wrapped in soft, rustling layers of tissue paper. Inside was a sweater of the softest and most beautiful cashmere she had ever seen, but the most stunning thing about it was the colour—it was a rich, vibrant violet, and she lifted it reverentially from the paper and held it against her cheek.

'Why, Poppy!' exclaimed Ella's mother, as she accepted a glass of sherry gratefully from her husband. 'What a gorgeous jersey—it matches your eyes exactly!'

Ella was by now examining the label. 'Good heavens, have you seen where he bought it? This must have cost the earth!'

'Oh, yes? Boyfriend, is it?' enquired Mrs Staunton mildly.

'My boss, actually,' corrected Poppy, going rather pink.

'Generous boss!' commented Mr Staunton drily.

Later, as they were all trudging down the icy lanes to work off the effects of their Christmas lunch, Ella managed to get Poppy on her own.

'Are you sure he's not sweet on you?' she asked.

'Who?'

'Who? The man who runs the wine bar, of course! Fergus bloody Browne, that's who!'

'Of course he isn't. He bought me a Christmas present, that's all.'

'Expensive present for a secretary. I reckon he's after you.'

'Oh, shut up, Ella! I keep telling you, he's already got a girlfriend.'

'Hmm,' pondered Ella. 'I wonder if she knows what he gave you for Christmas?'

It was a thought which had not escaped Poppy herself.

CHAPTER ELEVEN

THE period after Christmas was an anticlimax for most people, but not for Poppy. She had the forthcoming dermatology conference to fill her thoughts and most of her waking hours. It was also a convenient way of forgetting that she had still not told Fergus that she was planning to leave in the near future.

There never seemed a right time to tell him, and that wasn't helped by the fact that leaving was the last thing in the world she wanted to do. While she worked for him she could still dream—but Ella was right: she was only living her life in the shadows while she stayed with him.

She had rather awkwardly thanked him for the sweater, the realisation of just how much the gift must have cost making her both wistful yet embarrassed, and Fergus's response to her thanks had been equally stilted.

'That's OK,' he had muttered, wondering what had possessed him that day to walk into the most exclusive boutique in town and haltingly describe what he had wanted to buy. He recalled the rather tentative way in which the shop assistant had looked at him, informing him gently just how much such a garment would cost. And her expression of bemusement had changed to an all-knowing look when the man with the rather rumpled clothing had given her an all-encompassing, earth-shattering smile when she had produced the purple jumper for his appraisal. He had written a cheque for the huge sum immediately.

'You never can tell,' she had commented to her assistant after he had left. 'You just never can tell.'

Fergus had been disturbed by his recent behaviour, particularly over that overwhelming urge to kiss Poppy beneath the mistletoe. Thank goodness she'd been sensible enough to overlook it!

And he hadn't been sleeping well, either—he'd been as restless as a caged lion. He'd tried to ring Catherine a couple times, but she had never been there to receive his calls, and she hadn't returned them either. He couldn't understand why he didn't mind more. He was a man who had never laid much store by feelings or emotions. Sent away to boarding school at the age of seven, he hadn't really had anyone to discuss them with. He was the true scientist—logical and cool, with different compartments in his life for everything. Except that he hadn't felt particularly cool recently. Odd and disorientated would have been a better description, if he'd cared to think about it. But he didn't stop to think about it. As a scientist he never pondered on the imponderable. Vague feelings of disorientation were not facts. All he needed was a holiday. Things always tended to work themselves out, and, like Poppy, he found solace in work.

On the conference side, things could not have been going more swimmingly. With two nights to go, no speaker had yet pulled out. The drug company sponsoring it pronounced itself tremendously pleased with the coverage that their particular product would be receiving, and because their drug was one that Fergus liked and used frequently, he didn't feel that he was selling out by giving them that coverage.

'I've never been the type to be given trips to Athens, or accept a gold carriage clock from some rep selling a new "wonder drug" that's no different from any other on the market. But funding conferences or buying textbooks is an educational aid,' he told Poppy, and she nodded, wishing she could forget that kiss, that silly little kiss beneath the mistletoe.

Poppy had managed to get Fergus's friend Paul Burke to agree to come over. The day before the conference he rang from his home in Chicago, and she put him through to Fergus, watching a frown crease his forehead as he listened.

'Mmm,' he said. 'Could be tricky.' He looked up suddenly at Poppy, then said, 'Hold the line a minute, Paul. I may have found a solution.' He smiled at his secretary. 'Paul's wife has had to go away suddenly, which means that he'll have to bring his son. He's arranged for someone to take care of him during the day—a friend—but not for the evening—and he doesn't want to hire a total stranger. I was hoping that he and I could get together for dinner, and I was wondering. . .if you. . .'

She nodded, unable to refuse him anything when

he was looking at her like that. 'Babysit, you mean? Of course I'll do it. How old is he?'

Fergus flashed her a brilliant smile. 'Seven. He's seven. You're an angel, Poppy—I'll make it up to you!' He turned back to the receiver and began to talk excitedly to Paul.

I doubt it, she thought. The only way you could ever make it up would be to carry me off somewhere in true romantic fashion, and that was an empty dream.

After the conference. She must tell him after the conference: I'm going to leave you—after the conference.

The big day went without a hitch. Poppy was introduced to many eminent men and women whose names she had read on textbooks and papers on dermatology. Fergus spent most of the day beaming with pleasure, and insisted on Poppy joining himself and Paul at their table for lunch.

She liked the amusing man with the strange accent. Originally from Scotland, he had emigrated to the States after qualifying, and his speech was a combination of both those accents.

'Fergus and I became friends over the dissecting table,' he told Poppy, who winced slightly.

'Stop it, Paul,' remonstrated Fergus. 'You'll put her off her lunch!'

Poppy laughed. She certainly had little appetite, but the close proximity of her boss was far more responsible for that.

'Paul is the culprit who sends the ties I wear which I know you admire so much,' said Fergus, his eyes twinkling. 'Whenever he sees a particularly bizarre one, he sends it to me!'

'I had considered wearing my sunglasses to work,' said Poppy, and the two men laughed.

'What's the plan for tonight?' she asked. 'Does your son know who I am?'

'Sure,' replied Paul easily. 'I told him you were a friend of his godfather. Could you be at the hotel by about seven? Jay will go to sleep around eight—then I thought you could order yourself some dinner from room service.'

'Just make sure you choose the most expensive things on the menu!' joked Fergus.

'Have what you like, honey,' said Paul. 'I'm very grateful to you for stepping in like this. The lady he's with today was his nanny out in Chicago with us for a year, but she has her own family now, and I didn't want to have to ask her to work this evening as well.'

Poppy pushed her quiche to the side of her plate and stood up. 'I'd better get back,' she told them. 'I have to see the drug rep about this afternoon's running order.'

'But you've hardly touched your lunch!' protested Fergus.

'Skipping a meal won't hurt me—not after Christmas!' she replied. 'I'll see you later, Paul.'

'Fergus and I will pick you up around six-thirty, if that's all right?'

'Fine. Bye for now.'

They were both silent for a moment as she walked

away, the shiny bob of her hair sitting on the collar of her beautifully cut sage-green shirtwaister.

'She's a honey,' said Paul. 'You're lucky to have her.'

'I know,' said Fergus, that puzzled feeling of dejection filling him again as he watched Poppy retreat. Sometimes he felt more like a mixed-up schoolboy than an experienced man who had travelled the globe. What was the matter with him?

Paul was shaking him gently by the elbow. 'Say, Browne, you were miles away! Now tell me what's new. How's Catherine?'

The afternoon's presentations went just as smoothly. Fergus gave the closing talk, which was enthusiastically received, and then, to Poppy's horror, he said, 'I'd just like to thank my secretary, Poppy Henderson, for all her hard work. Without her, I don't think this conference would have been so well attended, or so beautifully arranged.'

All the audience followed the direction of his eyes to turn to look at her, and then started to clap loudly, and she stood there, her face scarlet.

She helped the caterers clear away the tea-things, and the drug reps to pack their stands and drug samples away, and by the time she was satisfied that the hall was as they had found it, it was almost six o'clock.

Ella wasn't at home, and there was barely time to have a swift shower and throw on a pair of jeans and a sweater before the doorbell rang.

She looked all warm and pink and clean, thought

Fergus as they waited while she threw a coat around her shoulders. She smelled of nothing more than soap, and yet it smelled better than any perfume.

Jay was a freckle-faced, lively seven-year-old who proudly showed Poppy a radio-cassette player.

'I got it for my birthday,' he told her in his strong American accent. 'Isn't it neat?'

'The best,' she assured him, and was rewarded with a grin.

'Say, you look pretty young—you don't happen to like. . .?' He mentioned the name of the latest group to hit the imagination of the pre-teen market and looked at her hopefully.

'Like them?' she exclaimed. 'I love them!'

'Great! Would you like to listen to their latest album?'

'Now don't you keep Miss Henderson up all night,' warned his father.

'Poppy,' she said firmly. 'I'd love to hear the album, and then Jay will go to bed, won't you, Jay?'

'You bet,' answered Jay happily.

But the evening did not go as planned. Jay went to bed after the music, but then began complaining that he felt unwell. Poppy wondered if he might be trying it on a bit, but when she felt his forehead he felt very hot. She removed the duvet and gave him a cold drink.

'How do you feel?' she asked, thankful that she'd taken the name of the restaurant that Fergus and Paul had gone to.

'Kinda weird,' he answered, in a small voice.

He vomited once, and she was just contemplating

ringing his father when she heard a key being turned in the door and there stood the two men.

'Fergus thought it wasn't fair. . .' began Paul when he took in the scene of Jay sitting on Poppy's lap, looking pale and miserable. He crossed the room quickly. 'Is he sick?' he asked anxiously.

'He's a bit hot, and was sick once,' answered Poppy. 'I couldn't find a thermometer.

'I have one,' said Paul. 'I can manage now. I'm sorry this had to happen. Come on, son—come to Daddy.' He lifted the child into his arms.

'Do you want us to stay?' asked Fergus, but Paul shook his head.

'I can manage—it's probably just a fever. And I'm probably qualified enough to look after him, even though I am a dermatologist! Did you miss supper, Poppy?'

'Yes, I did, but that's all right. I'm not particularly hungry.'

'You *are* going to eat,' said Fergus forcefully, helping her on with her coat. 'I'll ring you tomorrow, Paul. Goodbye, Jay—hope you're feeling better.'

'Thanks, Uncle Fergus,' muttered the boy.

Outside they waited while Fergus's car was brought round.

'I wonder what was the matter with him?' Poppy asked.

He shrugged. 'Probably just a bug, or the flu—there's a lot of illness around at this time of year.'

I know, she wanted to shout, I looked after you, didn't I? But she merely smiled.

'Where would you like to eat?' he asked.

'I'm not. . .' she began stubbornly.

'Oh, yes, you are,' he replied, equally stubbornly. 'No lunch, and now no supper. I'll be suspecting anorexia soon!'

'Oh, don't be so melodramatic,' she answered crossly. 'I'll have a sandwich at home.'

'I'm not sure I believe you,' he said. 'I'm offering to take you to a restaurant, for heaven's sake!'

And that was the last thing she wanted, a candlelit dinner with him.

'Look,' she told him patiently, 'you've already eaten. A restaurant won't be very pleased if you sit there having nothing. And I can't imagine you could manage to wade your way through another dinner!'

He opened the car door for her, then let himself in the driver's side. 'I wanted to thank you for all your hard work, Poppy.'

'Maybe some other time,' she lied. 'It's been a long day, and right now I'm longing for my bed.'

'Hmph,' he grunted, pressing his foot down on the accelerator.

They travelled in silence past the lighted shop windows, until Fergus suddenly stopped the car and began to get out.

'Wait there,' he ordered.

'Where are you going?' asked Poppy.

'You'll see,' he replied mysteriously, and was gone. He returned minutes later and thrust a warm paper bag into her hands.

'Eat that, Miss Henderson—or else!'

'What is it?'

'A hot dog,' he answered. 'And please don't tell

me you won't eat anything that isn't organic or covered in brown rice!'

'You must be joking!' The smell was absolutely mouthwatering. 'Just so long as you've put lots of greasy onions and tomato sauce in it!'

'The works,' he said, a smile on his lips.

He was right. She *was* starving and the hot dog tasted out of this world. Junk food it might be, but it satisfied her hunger admirably, and she hadn't been forced into a mock-romantic meal with him.

He stopped outside her flat, and she was half tempted to tell him she was leaving then, but it would have seemed churlish. She would wait until they were in the office. On Monday.

He turned off the engine. 'Do you want me to see you upstairs?' he asked.

She looked at him in surprise. He was far more chivalrous than most of the men she knew. 'No, of course not. I'll be fine. And anyway, my flatmate will be at home.'

'Of course.' He seemed to be waiting for something, and she was suddenly terrified that he'd give her a kiss, the kind of kiss that friends shared, like the Christmas kiss, and she couldn't handle it. He obviously had no idea of how he affected her.

'I'll see you on Monday,' she said hurriedly, getting out of the car. 'Goodnight.'

'Goodnight.'

He sat there until he saw a light appear at the window, before starting the engine up and roaring away. He could be very stubborn, Poppy thought as she heard him go.

Ella was not in. There was a note on the kitchen table.

>Gone to see Mum and Dad. With Andrew!!!
Back Sunday. Hope you've told old Fungus you're
leaving! Love, Ella X.

Poppy glowered and punched the cushion very hard. 'No, I haven't told him!' she shouted at the cushion. 'And what's more I don't want to tell him!'

She slept late next morning, sitting down after her bath to two pieces of thick wholemeal toast spread with runny honey and a cup of hot chocolate. Anorexic indeed! she thought crossly, as she took a huge bite.

She was just deciding what she should do for the rest of the weekend when the telephone began to ring, and she almost fell over when she heard Fergus's voice.

'Poppy? Are you still there?'

'Of course I am! Is anything wrong?'

'Well, yes and no. Paul rang this morning—Jay's covered in spots. He's got chicken-pox.'

'Chicken-pox!' she echoed.

'Have you had it? I have, and I assumed you probably had too. Poppy?'

'No—no,' she stammered, 'I haven't had it. None of us did, I remember Mama saying how lucky we'd all been.'

There was a pause. 'Not so lucky, really. It's far better to catch it as a child. You really ought not to come into contact with anyone else. You might not get it—the incubation period is ten to twenty-one days. If you get it you're infectious for about forty-eight hours before the spots come out, and then until they dry up. But you really must stay away from anyone who hasn't had it—it can be very nasty in adults.'

'Thanks for the words of encouragement!' She'd only been with Jay for a few hours—surely she wouldn't get it?

'Don't worry about it,' said Fergus contritely. 'You'll probably be safe—but you must ask your flatmate if she's had it. Can you do that now?'

'I can't!' wailed Poppy. 'She's away.'

'Find out, then—and ring me back, will you?'

'OK.'

She phoned Ella's parents and Ella answered. 'My parents love him,' she hissed as her opening gambit.

'Who?' asked Poppy, taken aback.

'Andrew, of course! My father's taking him golfing this afternoon.'

Poppy remembered why she had rung. Ella, it transpired, had not had chicken-pox either.

'Don't worry,' she told her. 'I'll sort something out. I wouldn't dream of giving it to you!'

'I should think not!'

She rang Fergus back and told him.

'I'm coming round,' was all he said. And he rang off.

He arrived ten minutes later. 'I've found the perfect solution,' he announced. 'You can come and stay with me!'

CHAPTER TWELVE

'I CAN'T do that,' Poppy told him flatly.

'Why not? It seems to me the perfect solution. I won't even be there for a lot of the time—next week I'm flying to Oslo, remember? You can still do my work from there, I can bring clinic tapes home for you, and while I'm away, you can continue with my manuscript. If you do get it you'll only feel lousy for a couple of days—and there's no need for you to see anyone else and risk infecting them. Now what possible objection can you have to that?'

Poppy couldn't possibly give him her real reason for being so reluctant to share his house. And it was true—she had nowhere else to go. She couldn't fly home to Ireland and risk giving it to other people on the way there. And if he was going away. . .

'OK,' she nodded reluctantly, 'I'll come. Ella's not back until tomorrow evening—I'll come then.'

'I'll come and pick you up before she arrives. About five?'

'Yes, five.'

He really did seem most concerned about her welfare, she thought as he fired a barrage of questions at her. Did she want him to do any shopping for her? Was there anything she needed? Books? Magazines?

150

'I'm *all right*,' she told him. 'I'll see you tomorrow at five.'

After he had gone, she thought she must have had a brainstorm, agreeing to go like that. But what alternative did she have?

The following day Fergus arrived promptly at five, and helped her into the car as gingerly as if she were already an invalid.

She turned to him. 'Now listen, Fergus,' she said firmly. 'I'm not ill yet, thank you, so you can take the kid gloves off right now!'

He laughed, feeling disturbingly lighthearted. 'Consider them removed!'

When they arrived, Poppy saw—to her astonishment—that the house was clean, no dishes heaped up in the sink, no great piles of papers and books.

'This looks tidy!' she exclaimed, and he actually flashed her a grateful look.

'You—um—I've put you—er—I mean—you know which is your bedroom?' he asked gruffly. 'The one you had. . .'

'Yes, yes,' she interposed hastily, willing the blush not to creep into her cheeks. If they were going to be walking on eggshells like this the whole time, then her stay there was going to be a disaster. But the evening passed pleasantly and uneventfully. Fergus went out for a Chinese meal and showed her how to make little pancake parcels containing duck, spring onion, cucumber and plum sauce. Then they ate sesame prawn toast which Poppy pronounced delicious, as was the ice-cold Canadian lager which he produced to accompany it.

After supper he showed her the manuscript in his study, and the rather ancient typewriter he used.

'Do as much of it as you can,' he said. 'I'll be back from Oslo next Sunday evening. Make yourself at home—I've stocked the freezer and all the cupboards up with food and fruit and vegetables. There's wine in the dining-room.' There was a pause. The light from the lamp on his desk had bathed them in a soft golden pool. Poppy could hear the loud ticking of her watch, could see the brilliance of his grey eyes, and the shadows on his face.

'I think I'll go up now—I could fall asleep on my heels! Will I see you in the morning?'

He shook his head. 'My flight leaves at seven— I'll be up with the larks. Goodnight, Poppy.'

'Goodnight, Fergus.

In the morning, when she awoke, she felt as though she was existing in some kind of surreal state. In his guest-room. In his house. But no sign of Fergus. The watch she had left on the bedside table read 9.45—he must have left hours ago.

It was the most curious position to be in—she couldn't go out, and she saw no one. By day she typed up his manuscript, and after a long bath she would settle herself down beside the fire, eschewing both television and radio, choosing instead one of the many books that lined his study walls. The cat lay curled up beside her feet, purring to complete the perfect scene of domestic bliss. She knew it was wishful thinking, but she felt so right being there— almost as if it were her spiritual home. Silly Poppy, she mused, poking the fire so that vivid orange sparks startled the cat—you want far, far too much.

Twice Fergus rang, and the second time he began babbling on excitedly about a new systemic antibiotic which was due soon to be tested on humans.

'It's remarkable, Poppy!' he exclaimed. 'Well, all the results are extremely encouraging.' Then he started talking about 'broad spectrum' and 'a possibility of reduced tinnitus and thrush' or at least that was what she *thought* he'd said, but he was talking so quickly and in such technical detail that she couldn't be sure.

And then he said, 'I'm sorry, Poppy—for a minute I forgot. . .'

'Forgot what?' she queried, bemused, but the money had obviously run out and the line went dead.

Fergus stood grinning inanely at the glacial beauty who sat behind the reception desk. 'I forgot she wasn't a doctor!' he said wonderingly, to no one in particular, and went over to find the rest of his group.

He had told her he would be home at around six-thirty on the Sunday evening. She couldn't wait.

Would it seem over the top if she cooked something for them? What if he'd already eaten on the plane? She dithered around all day, before deciding on a casserole with baked potatoes and salad. If he had already eaten then it would keep—and she still had to eat herself, for goodness' sake!

Once, when she was chopping up a sprig of thyme from his herb garden, she felt a wave of dizziness wash over her, producing a fleeting moment of nausea, but it had gone so quickly that she thought she must have imagined it.

She had just finished crushing a clove of garlic into the vinaigrette dressing when she heard the sound of his key, and instinctively she rushed into the hall, grinning all over her face, to see him putting his case down, a wide smile on his lips and a look of pleasure in his eyes. They stood there gaping at one another.

'You're back!' she exclaimed foolishly.

He didn't seem to notice that she'd stated the obvious, the smile was still there. 'Yes, indeed. Are you well?' He sniffed appreciatively. 'What's that wonderful smell?'

'Casserole.' She was shy now. 'Unless you ate on the plane?'

He shuddered. 'I never eat on planes.' The grey eyes twinkled. 'Do you?'

'There's never really time between London and Ireland.' Poppy forced her voice to be light, but she didn't know what to say to him; it seemed too gloriously intimate to be welcoming him back from a trip abroad. She struggled to find something to say about work.

'I'm halfway through your book,' she told him.

Fergus stared at her blankly. 'My book?'

'Your manuscript, of course!' she explained.

'Yes, of course.' He shook his head a little as if forcing himself back to the present. 'I'd like to go and shower and change. Will your casserole wait?'

'My casseroles go on for hours!'

'It will be interesting to see if you're as good a cook as you are a secretary,' he murmured, and she was glad that he was halfway up the stairs, for it stopped him seeing the colour that had crept into her cheeks at his compliment.

But her cheeks continued to burn as she walked into the kitchen and lit a flame underneath the carrots. She began to set two places at the large pine table on which stood a large vase of winter twigs, but the sound of the cutlery clattering proved oddly intrusive. By the time Fergus reappeared, wearing a light grey sweater and a pair of grey cords, she felt distinctly cotton-woolly.

'Would you like some wine. . .?' he began, then frowned and crossed the kitchen quickly. 'No,' he said decisively, 'you wouldn't. What's the matter, Poppy—you look awful?'

'I—I——' she stammered, but before she could piece together a reply she heard him exclaim something, then catch hold of her shoulders.

'Come over here,' he said, pulling her underneath the light and peering down at her. Then, 'Good grief—you've got it! You've definitely caught it!'

'Caught what?' His face seemed to be dancing before her eyes like a marionette.

'Chicken-pox, of course!' He shook his head from side to side. 'Textbook stuff! Exactly ten days' incubation—you've two spots on your neck and I expect you'll be covered in them by tomorrow!'

'Don't!' Poppy groaned.

'Oh, don't worry,' he replied cheerfully. 'You'll feel lousy for a day or two, but then you'll be fine.

You'll probably even feel like finishing off my manuscript!'

'Slavedriver,' she muttered, wishing her legs didn't feel like jelly that hadn't quite set properly.

'It's off to bed with you, young lady,' Fergus announced briskly.

She felt hot and sweaty and strangely obsinate. 'What about supper?' she asked.

'Stuff supper!' he growled, in as forthright a tone as she'd ever heard from him. 'You're obviously going to fall over in a moment. Come here.'

And before she could try to stop him, even though she had hardly the strength to brush a fly from her arm, he had scooped her up in his arms and was carrying her up the stairs. But he didn't carry her to her customary guest-room, instead she found herself deposited in the centre of his large soft bed.

She looked up in alarm. 'But I don't. . .'

'Don't worry, I'm not planning to use your fevered state to take advantage of you. But you're ill and you can have the best bed—we'll swap.'

'Oh,' she said faintly, feeling muddled, her lips all dry. 'No kissing this time, though.'

Fergus was staring at her with a bemused expression. What was she talking about? 'I assume that you have a nightdress or something next door?'

Poppy nodded with a head growing increasingly heavy. 'Uh-huh.'

'Then just get yourself undressed and under that sheet while I fetch it for you.'

But when he returned carrying a short nightshirt,

she had flopped into the middle of the bed where he'd left her.

He shook her shoulder gently. 'Wake up, Poppy,' he urged.

'Fergus!' she murmured dreamily.

His reply was a terse expletive before he unzipped her jeans and pulled them down. He divested her of her sweater equally roughly, trying all the time to keep his eyes averted, but when he came to unclip the lacy bra, and the lush, firm young breasts came spilling out, it was as much as he could do not to exclaim aloud. Poppy's eyes flew open.

'Fergus?' she whispered tentatively.

'Save your breath for getting better,' he snapped in a gruff, abrupt voice, but when he saw her look of consternation his tone softened. 'Stop worrying, will you? I'm just getting you into bed.'

'Mmm,' she sighed, and closed her eyes again as she leaned against him, and he muttered something underneath his breath.

He pulled the nightshirt over her head and covered her to mid-thigh. That would have to do. Doctor or no doctor, he didn't feel able to remove the brief matching lacy pants she wore.

He pulled the sheet up to her neck and stood looking down at her, listening to her hoarse breathing. Her shiny hair fanned his pillow and he had never felt quite so protective in his whole life. Fool!

'I'll fetch you some aspirin,' he said, and turned on his heel and left the room.

CHAPTER THIRTEEN

How right he was! Was he ever wrong about anything? Poppy wondered. Within two days she was
sitting up, eating everything he put before her, and
was feeling very comfortable indeed.

He'd come in one morning with her tea, an odd
expression on his face, and had said gruffly, 'If
you're wondering how you came to be undressed
and put into bed, it was me—you weren't fit for
anything.'

She gave a smile, her Irish accent more pronounced, as it always was when she was embarrassed. 'Sure, and aren't you the doctor, now?'

Fergus laughed, remembering that he had not felt
in the least bit professional, and he knew for a fact
that he certainly wouldn't be able to treat her. But
then she wasn't his patient, was she? She was his
secretary, and his friend. Perhaps it was a good thing
that he was out all day at the hospital.

He should have been tired and foul-tempered, but
he wasn't. The wards were frantic, a baby died of
epidermolysis bullosa, which upset everyone, and
then, to cap it all, Geoff told him he was leaving to
go to work in Saudi Arabia.

'But why, Geoff, man? You're the best charge
nurse this ward has ever had,' asked Fergus in
despair.

Geoff looked sad. 'I don't want to go, but what else can I do? I'm a married man, Fergus. Glenda wants to have a baby within the next couple of years and we just can't afford to on my salary alone. We can't even afford to buy a bedsit at the moment, for heaven's sake!'

Fergus shook his head. 'Then why won't they pay nurses more?' he demanded savagely. 'We're losing all our best people.'

Yet when he walked through his front door at the end of the day, his worries seemed to fade into insignificance—she was so good to come home to.

By the fourth day he found Poppy up and dressed sitting at the typewriter when he came home.

'You look better,' he told her approvingly. 'Sure you're up to it?'

'Fit as a flea,' she answered. 'I'm just about finished now.'

'Go and sit by the fire and I'll bring your supper through on a tray.'

They were living in a vacuum, a world where no one else existed. A curiously relaxed state had overcome Poppy. It was as though she had forgotten how deep her feelings for him ran; perhaps she had shut out thoughts of how attractive she found him for her own safety. Instead, they were locked together in pure harmony, living and working side by side. She wanted it never to end. But she knew that all things must end.

By the time her spots had dried up she had begun to feel restless, longing to go for a long walk, but unwilling to shatter the perfection of their isolation.

That morning Fergus said to her over breakfast.
'Wrap up warmly—I'm going to take you out in the
car.'

She took him at his word and flew upstairs, piling
on layers of clothing beneath her windcheater, as
well as scarf, mittens and a woolly hat. She had
spent many afternoons wandering around the wild
splendour of the large gardens attached to the back
of the house, but now she wanted a change of scene.

'Good grief,' he said, when he saw her. 'I'd
planned a day on the coast—did you think we'd be
climbing Ben Nevis?'

Poppy strapped herself into his car, snuggling
down happily and wriggling her toes in their warm
boots. She knew that the spots were almost clear
and soon she would no longer be infectious, and
then she would have to leave, not just his house, but
his employ too. But just for today she was going to
pretend. Pretend he cared for her in the same way.
Pretend they were in love and were going to spend a
wonderful day out together, just like any other
young couple. Pretending. There was no harm in
pretending.

They drove to Brighton and parked the car, then
walked along the pier, the cold wind whirling round
them and blowing all the cobwebs away. The grey
sea rose up in high waves, with foamy white crests
atopping each. A lone fisherman stood, silent as a
statue, and eager seagulls made swooping circles
around him.

After the pier, they explored the Lanes, investi-
gating every antique shop. Poppy's attention was

caught by an exquisite amethyst pendant, its pale purple fire sparkling and contrasting with a gold chain so fine it appeared to be just a sliver of light. She browsed through a catalogue while Fergus bought himself an ancient set of fire-tongs—the tongs themselves looking perfectly normal until you peered a little more closely to find that they were the expertly fashioned wings of a bat.

They had lunch in a small pub, where great logs lay smouldering, heaped in a recessed fireplace. Fergus bought her a schooner of sherry which was liquid gold when held to the light of the flickering flames, then they tucked into substantial portions of piping hot shepherd's pie.

Eventually Poppy pushed her dish aside and sighed. 'That was scrumptious! I've eaten so much I really don't think I can move.'

The grey eyes twinkled. 'You don't have to. We're in no hurry. Sit there and sip your drink and think about how you'd like to put the world to rights!'

She felt emboldened by the lunchtime drink. 'So how did you come to have an Irish name?' she asked, and he smiled.

'My mother,' he explained, 'was a woman in love with Irish mythology.

'And what does the "C" stand for?'

'Connor,' he admitted.

'Connor!' She grinned delightedly. 'Imagine that!'

They lapsed into silence, but never had silence left her feeling so totally at peace, so that when eventually they left the pub, she felt as though she were drifting along on a cloud of happiness.

She fell asleep on the way back, and by the time they pulled up outside the Edwardian villa it had grown completely dark.

Stepping back into the silent, cold house, she felt the dream disperse a little.

'Perhaps I'd better go and do some packing,' she said awkwardly. 'I'll have to be thinking about going. . .'

'Shush!' Fergus interrupted her. 'It's been such a perfect day—I don't want to spoil it. Just for once, let's not live in the future, or the past. Let's just enjoy the present.'

It was so unlike the sort of thing that he normally would have said that it was as though he had guessed her fantasy and was entering into it. Poppy looked up at him with shining eyes and nodded.

'I'm going to cook supper for us tonight,' he told her. 'To make up for that time when you wouldn't let me buy you more than a hot dog!'

'Then I'll go and change,' she said shyly.

Not that she had much to change into. She bathed and washed her hair, then surveyed the few garments which she'd brought with her. And there, lying in solitary splendour in one of the drawers, she saw her violet sweater. She had never worn it— there had never seemed to be a right time to wear it. Until now.

The glorious softness clung to her top like a second skin. She pulled on a knee-length black skirt and black shoes and dusted her eyes with violet shadow, but she wore no lipstick. Lipstick would have been all wrong—too contrived.

When eventually she surveyed herself in the mirror she saw a tall, slim yet curvy young woman with shiny eyes and cheeks which were pink with excitement. The outfit could have done with some adornment—but still, you couldn't have everything.

She came down the stairs slowly, and there he was in the hall, staring at her as if he couldn't believe his eyes. He too had changed, looking even more assured and elegant than he had on the night of the party, if that were possible. Was this really Fergus? she asked herself, until she saw the glint in those mercurial grey eyes and that untamed lock of light golden brown hair which still flopped on to his forehead.

She felt as high as a kite, but she accepted his glass of champagne gratefully, glad to have something to do with hands that threatened to shake and tremble like a leaf in the wind.

The evening passed as though in a dream. Vaguely Poppy was aware that Fergus had prepared a light but delicious supper—salmon, followed by strawberries—where on earth had he managed to find strawberries at this time of year?

He cosseted her and spoiled her, and flirted with her. He was definitely flirting with her. At first she thought she must be mistaken, then, when she was sure, she began to flirt back.

They were engaged in a long, slow game, one as old as time itself. For tonight he was no longer Fergus, her boss, the occasionally intimidating man she had grown to like and love. And she was not

Poppy, his devoted secretary, who unbeknown to him had for weeks now been craving what she had always imagined was the unimaginable—an attachment which to all their peers would always be considered unsuitable: the typist and the consultant. Laughable, really—like *The Prince and the Showgirl*. Unreal and unworkable.

But tonight none of that mattered. Tonight they were simply a man and a woman caught up in Nature's own special kind of magic, drawn together by an invisible thread, and she dared not analyse it, for fear that it would simply disappear.

'I have something for you,' Fergus told her.

'For me?'

He handed her a small blue box and she looked at him with puzzled eyes. 'Go on, open it.'

Inside was the amethyst pendant which she had admired so much in the Lanes that day. She looked up at him with starry eyes.

'It's beautiful,' she said simply. 'Thank you.'

'Shall I help you put it on.'

'Yes, please.'

He stood and fastened the chain, his hand lightly brushing the back of her neck as he did so. When he had finished he gently propelled her forward, so that she stood in front of the mirror. The necklace sparkled and glittered, reflecting the deeper mauve of the sweater and her eyes.

Her gaze moved up from the necklace to his reflected face, and their eyes met and held for a long moment.

'Poppy. . .' Fergus's voice was husky as he bent to

kiss the back of her neck with a slow, sensuous movement, and she began to tremble as she saw their reflection in the mirror. It seemed to take an hour before he finally turned her round and brushed his mouth against hers, and she kissed him back with a heartfelt sigh of longing. No kiss had ever been so perfect, and he was holding on to her so tightly, like a man who had been dying of thirst and who had suddenly been put before the purest, coolest well of water.

And if ever she had wondered for what purpose she had been put on the earth, she now knew. It had been to be in Fergus's arms like this, to kiss him back with a passion that overwhelmed her, to feel his heart beat close to her.

'Poppy,' he breathed. 'All day I've been thinking of this, dreaming of this. . .' He lifted his head, a question in his eyes. 'Do you want this, my darling? We can stop now. . .?'

'No,' she whispered, powerless in his arms to deny what she wanted more than anything else.

Not another word was spoken as he took her by the hand and led her upstairs to his room. And there was no pretence, no coyness or games as he moved with her towards the bed.

She had never known that it could take so long for a man to undress a woman. He was making her wait, and it was exquisite agony. Only once, as he deliciously peeled down the filmy fabric of her stockings, and his hand brushed lightly against her inner thigh, did she gasp his name aloud, and she saw him smile, a secret smile.

And when she was naked he ripped his own clothes off, throwing them to the floor with careless disregard, as though he couldn't wait to be rid of them. Poppy felt the bed sink slightly as he moved next to her, and began to kiss her once more, his warm nakedness filling her with eager, trembling anticipation. And her arms came up to encircle his neck, aching with need, longing to begin this, the greatest adventure of her life.

In the morning Fergus propped himself up on one elbow and looked silently down at her still sleeping form, her cheeks pinker than usual, the bright, soft hair looking more tousled than he had ever seen it. In a minute he would wake her in the most satisfactory way he knew, but not yet.

Just for a minute longer he wanted to drink in the sheer beauty of her.

This, then. This was what it was all about. This the feeling that men had died for, that countless poems and plays, sonnets and songs had been written about. Governments had toppled, great rulers had relinquished power for this overwhelming passion which had seized him with such surprising force. Love. He had been blind not to realise what had been happening to him before. He could kill for her.

He bent his head to her shoulder, to kiss the satin softness of her skin, when the bleeping of the telephone halted him. He picked up the phone immediately, lest it should wake her.

'Hi, Fergus,' said a voice which had grown strangely unfamiliar. 'It's Catherine.'

Catherine! He sat up quickly.

'Fergus?' Are you still there?'

Unconsciously he had lowered his voice. 'Yes, I'm still here. Can you hold on—I'll take this in the study.'

As soon as she heard the door close quietly behind her, Poppy opened her eyes. She had heard every word. There was a feeling of sick dread in her stomach, a real pain in her heart. And a growing knot of some new, violent anger.

She scrambled out of bed and without thinking ran silently to the other room, throwing on her old jeans and sweater, piling the few clothes she had into the small case. She forced herself to go back into Fergus's bedroom and to pick her skirt, stockings and underwear from the floor where they lay beneath his trousers. The sweater she left in a crumpled heap. She never wanted to see the thing again.

She caught the tail end of the conversation as she came down the stairs.

'. . . Yes, of course I'll see you, but it can't be today. . . All right—tomorrow. . . That's fine.'

She heard him replacing the receiver as she reached the bottom of the stairs, saw him come out of the study, his face lost in thought.

When he saw her there, fully dressed, she saw the emotions crossing his face puzzlement, disconcertion. And guilt. Definitely guilt. He hurried towards her, the dark towelling dressing-gown affording her a view of the muscular chest, and, shamefully, she knew a wave of desire.

'Darling. . .' he began, but her words cut across him.

'Don't "darling" me,' she said coldly. 'It was Catherine on the phone, wasn't it?'

'Poppy, let me explain.'

The pain was twisting inside her. She nodded. 'Very well. Explain just one thing—are you and Catherine still an "item", as they say?'

'She. . .'

'A yes or no will do, Fergus,' she snapped.

He looked helpless. 'It isn't as easy as that.'

The anger erupted like a volcano. The words tumbled out before she could stop them. 'I'll bet it isn't! So you went to bed with me last night. Does Catherine know? Perhaps she just turns a blind eye to your little dalliances. How many women do you sleep with, Fergus? Did you have someone in Oslo last week, and isn't it rather risky in this day and age?'

His face had gone white. 'If you think that,' he said in a voice filled with icy distaste, 'then I think you'd probably better go.'

She had thought she had seen him angry before, but any rages had been nothing compared to the way he was regarding her now; the contempt in his eyes was enough to make her cringe.

Without another word she picked up her case and tore out of the front door, running down the street like a crazy woman. She couldn't stop the tears, or the great sobs which were tearing from her chest.

Several people stared at her anxiously; one even tried to catch her arm. 'Are you all right, dear.' But she shook the hand away.

She hadn't wanted to see anyone, but the sight of James West, crossing the road towards her, was too much to resist. Dropping her case on to the pavement, she fell into his arms and sobbed the most broken tears he had ever heard.

CHAPTER FOURTEEN

THE job was the worst imaginable, far worse than Ella's jokes about offices right at the beginning. The office was tiny and windowless—unless you counted the dusty skylight which was meshed by bars to prevent break-ins. As if anyone would want to break into that prison of a place.

Poppy's boss was called Barry, and he was young, unscrupulous and unsavoury. His hair was too long, and he drove a sports car and spent much of the day making lewd suggestions to Poppy, who pretended not to hear them. And at least he was so insensitive that he didn't even notice her red-rimmed eyes or solemn manner. His business was selling office stationery over the telephone. Apparently it was what was known as 'cold' selling.

As far as Poppy could make out, this basically meant telling people a lot of lies. He sold carbon paper at grossly inflated prices, simply because he had the gift of the gab. A lot of companies then rang up to complain, and part of Poppy's job was to field these complaints. Barry was in to no one.

The other part of her job was to get the carbon paper off to customers, type the invoices, make Barry his sickly-sweet coffee and try not to think about Fergus. The latter was the one she found most difficult to do.

How could she stop thinking about him, after what had happened? Yet none of her thoughts made sense. Had she misjudged him? Because he just hadn't seemed the type of man to have a quick fling with his secretary while his girlfriend was away. She had assumed that it was all over between him and Catherine.

So why hadn't she asked him before she went to bed with him? a small voice tormented her. Was it because she was afraid of what the answer would be?

And why had he been so secretive when Catherine rang, if he'd had nothing to hide? Why had he been so evasive when she had challenged him? Perhaps these interludes of casual sex were par for the course in his odd relationship with Catherine, in which case Poppy had misjudged him badly. And perhaps if she hadn't made herself so blatantly available, then the whole incident might never have happened.

Or was she just being naïve in supposing that there was anything more than the one night they had shared? How had he put it? 'Let's not live in the future, or the past. Let's just enjoy the present.' Maybe he had meant it literally and, unlike Catherine, she was no part of his past, or his future.

In bleak, dark nights she reminded herself that even if there had been a reasonable explanation, which seemed unlikely, that a man like Fergus would be unable to forgive her for all the hateful things she had accused him off.

But still she hoped. She wore his necklace carefully hidden beneath her sweater like a talisman which would bring him back to her.

She automatically winced as Barry lit yet another cigarette and blew the smoke in rings across the office, which for some reason always made him snort with barely suppressed hysteria. Still, she had to be thankful that she had her job. It paid the rent, and she was lucky that Miss Webb had employed her at all.

Miss Humphries, the head of medical secretaries, had been nonplussed when she had spoken to her old friend Miss Webb on the telephone.

'I've spoken to him and he's told me it would be "impossible" for them to continue working together,' she had said. 'I just don't understand it—they were getting along famously.'

'There's more to this than meets the eye,' Miss Webb had replied darkly.

Poppy had been heartbroken when she had heard of Fergus's words through Miss Webb, and that evening she took off the amethyst necklace and pushed it to the back of a drawer.

To make it worse, Miss Webb had been unable to hide her irritation from Poppy—because the girl had steadfastly refused both other medical secretarial jobs offered to her.

'Miss Humphries thinks you're excellent—please won't you reconsider?' she had pleaded, but Poppy had been adamant. She was *not* going to work anywhere where there was the remotest chance she might bump into Fergus Browne.

Which was why she must think herself lucky to have a regular income, even if it was sitting in a gloomy office working for the ghastly Barry with his erroneous idea that she might be interested in going for a drink after work with him.

Ella, though initially sympathetic, had eventually taken her moping flatmate to task.

'Why did you do it, Poppy? *Why*? And you, of all people!'

Because I love him, thought Poppy bleakly, but said nothing as she excused herself and disappeared into the bathroom for a long bath.

James had been wonderful that day—he had taken her home, had sat and listened while she sobbed, had made her hot, sweet tea and had asked her one question only.

'Do you want to talk about it?'

'No!' she wailed. 'I'm sorry, James, but I just can't.' How could she tell him that she'd had a stupid, unthinkable one-night stand with their boss? She had been the foolish one—there was no need to discredit Fergus in James's eyes.

James had looked at her thoughtfully and shrugged. 'That's up to you,' he had said. 'But you know where I am if you need me.'

Life continued in the same dismal pattern for the next two weeks, until Poppy arrived home to find Ella waiting for her.

'There's been a phone call for you,' she said, and Poppy caught her breath instinctively.

'Not. . .?'

Ella scowled. 'No, definitely not—and if it had been, I don't think I'd have told you.'

Poppy managed a half-hearted smile.

'A Mrs West—she said she'll call back,' Ella went on.

'West?' frowned Poppy. 'I don't know a Mrs West.'

'James's mother, she said. And she sounded—oh, I don't know. Very strange.'

Mrs West rang back within the half-hour.

'Miss Henderson?' she began, and her voice sounded close to tears. 'I understand you're a friend of my son—James.' The story came pouring out. James had caught chicken-pox. The side-effect in adults was rare, but James had succumbed to it. The chicken-pox virus had entered his lungs, and he was at present fighting for his life in the intensive care unit.

'The doctors are doing all they can,' she said tremulously. 'But they told us to try anything. His flatmate told us he was very fond of you, and we thought—we wondered. . .' Her voice faded away doubtfully.

'I'll come and see him straight away,' said Poppy decisively. 'Where is he?'

'At your hospital—where you met. He's at Highchester.'

Highchester. Poppy walked towards the tall, lighted building and shivered. She hadn't been there for over a month, and the associations of the place with Fergus were still overwhelmingly strong.

Except that now there was another far more serious association: James was lying in there gravely ill—and it was all her fault.

She made her way to the intensive care unit, and spoke quietly to the sister who greeted her.

'Is Mrs West here? Would it be possible to see her?'

'I'll find out. Your name. . .?'

'Is Henderson—Poppy Henderson.'

Mrs West came quite quickly. She looked very like James, with the same crisp blonde curls, though streaks of grey were unmistakable.

She had the same dazzling blue eyes too, but Poppy thought that those eyes must have been doing quite a lot of crying recently. She drew in a deep breath, to give her courage for what she must say.

'I'm afraid I'm the one responsible for your son's illness. It was me who gave him the chicken-pox. I was supposed to be in isolation, but. . .but. . .'

To her amazement, the older woman was shaking her head. 'But we knew that, my dear—his flatmate told us you'd gone down with it. You mustn't blame yourself. The doctors say chicken-pox is a virus which is always around us, and that if he hadn't caught it from you, he could have caught it from someone else. He was just. . .just. . .' and here her voice cracked a little, and faded to almost a whisper so that Poppy had to strain to hear her words, '. . . very unfortunate.'

Poppy blinked back her tears. How could this kind woman be so generous? 'Please. . .' she said. 'Please, may I go and see him now?'

Mrs Webb nodded and motioned her into a small changing-room, where Poppy had to put on a gown, clogs and mask. Outside the cubicle they paused.

'Why don't you go and get yourself some tea or something?' said Poppy. 'I'll stay with him until you get back.'

The white-faced woman nodded gratefully, squeezed Poppy's hand for a brief moment, then walked away.

A nurse was by his bedside, and she was immediately aware of the strange-sounding hissing noise. Silently she walked over to the bed and looked down at him. He had been intubated. He was on a ventilator. He was unable to breathe for himself and a machine was having to do it for him.

She sat down beside him and took one hand into her own. 'It's Poppy, James,' she said aloud, without even realising that she had done so. 'I've come to help you get better.'

But he didn't get better. His condition worsened. He was critically ill—she could see it in the faces of the doctors who buzzed in and out of the cubicle. There seemed to be an awful lot of consultants by his bed. And where there had been just one nurse, there were now two, and sometimes three.

Poppy went to see him whenever she could. The nurses got quite used to her rushing to the hospital straight from work, often relieving his parents so that they could grab a bite of supper. Or she would sit quietly in the small coffee-room designed for visitors to the unit. Waiting, always waiting. Just in case.

That weekend she was barely out of the place, she somehow felt that by keeping a vigil, she could will James to live.

On the Sunday evening, while his parents had made a brief visit home to collect some clean clothes to bring in, he took a turn for the worse. The nurse began speeding up a drip, while another stared at some dials in alarm.

'Get the consultant and call his parents at home. Get them back,' the first instructed the other briskly, and she sped off.

Poppy felt supernumerary, unwilling to leave, but uncertain whether she could stay.

'Am I in the way?' she appealed helplessly to the nurse. 'Is there anything I can do?'

'Talk to him. Until the team arrives—talk to him. Sweet-talk him or something. You never know.'

Poppy placed her warm hand, so full of life, over his still one.

'You're gorgeous, James,' she whispered. 'Just about the nicest man I've ever known—the sweetest, kindest man I've ever known.'

She was scarcely aware of the tall figure who paused very briefly in the doorway before moving quickly across to the bed, and then some second sense warned her, and she looked up to find Fergus drawing up a syringe full of drugs which he then began to inject into the giving set of the drip.

'You'd better leave now, Poppy,' he said gruffly. 'We're going to be very busy in here.'

As if in reply to his words, she heard running footsteps, and about four doctors piled into the room, all with tight, anxious faces.

She quickly got to her feet and stumbled blindly

out of the door, but no one noticed her go, they were too intent on saving the life of James West.

Mr and Mrs West appeared and sat silently in the coffee-room with her, holding each other's hands tightly. They seemed to have shrunk by several inches since they had left to go home.

Never had time passed more slowly. Each time Poppy looked at the clock it seemed that only one more minute had passed instead of the hour it had felt like. Please let him live, God, I'd give you anything I could, if you'd just let James live.

A figure stood there, his eyes flicking over her before they came to rest on Mr and Mrs West, who got nervously to their feet.

His face was still serious, but it suddenly broke into the most beautiful smile, and Poppy let out a sigh of relief, knowing that he was the bearer of good, not bad news.

'He's improving—he seems to have survived the crisis.' Fergus spoke quietly, but she could see the fear leave the Wests' eyes.

'You can come down and see him now.'

She knew that the invitation excluded her, but she didn't care. She was just incredibly happy for James and his parents, and relieved, too, that she could now escape from the awful reality of how much Fergus despised her.

She was exhausted—so tired that the thought of the journey home was intolerable just then. After Fergus had left with the Wests, she made her way to the visitors' canteen; at least she wouldn't meet anyone she knew in there.

She drank some coffee and sat there for some time, feeling like a zombie, unable to face the decisions which she would now inevitably have to make. Because she had been nurturing some tiny flicker of hope in her heart that perhaps she and Fergus still had some chance together. Today she had discovered that that hope was now completely dead, she had read it in the coldness of his eyes, and she could not ever bear to see him look at her in such a way again.

It was now almost half-past nine. She stood up to leave, but with the curious sense of detachment which had overwhelmed her since she had left the intensive care unit. Without thinking, she found that her feet had taken her to the corridor where she had once worked, almost to the room itself. She had once been happy here. Mad, mad fool, she mentally chided herself—but at least this time Fergus wouldn't be there. She could risk it.

But as she passed his office, she saw to her horror that the door was partially open and that a figure sat at the desk, an anglepoise light on. It must be Fergus, she thought in dread, as she instinctively began to walk on tiptoe and increase her pace slightly—but even as she did so she heard a chair scrape against the floor, and footsteps.

Please don't let him see me, she prayed—don't make me appear a desperate fool. But her prayers went unanswered as she heard the distinctive timbre of his voice as he called her name.

She couldn't just run away, that would just be childish, so reluctantly she turned to face him.

He moved towards her, his grey eyes fixed on her face, and she was stricken with such longing and embarrassment that she could hardly meet his gaze.

He stopped a few inches away from her, and her body instinctively knew a shiver of response to the proximity of his. What the hell did he want? she wondered, knowing only that this closeness, without any of the closeness they had previously shared, was like a kick in the teeth.

'I just wanted to say. . .' His voice faltered, and he began again. 'I was very rude to you in the unit earlier, and I wanted the chance to apologise. I'm sorry, Poppy.'

She didn't dare speak, for fear she might cry, but it seemed that Fergus had more to say.

'And I'm so glad that James is on the mend.'

'Yes,' she agreed. 'It's wonderful news.'

'And I hope you'll both be very happy.' The words seemed to cost him a lot of effort to say properly.

Poppy lifted her eyebrows. 'Very happy? What on earth are you talking about?'

'Oh, come off it, Poppy!' His voice sounded strained. 'Everyone's talking about it. The vigil you kept by his bedside. And I heard you myself—the way you were talking to him.'

She was astounded, then angry. He must know there was nothing between them. How could there be? He was simply searching for the easy answer— well, she wasn't going to give him the easy answer! 'I've been praying for him to get better.' Her voice broke. 'Don't you think I felt guilty enough as it was? If I hadn't. . .if we hadn't. . .then I'd never have given him the chicken-pox in the first place. And did you really think I could transfer my affections so quickly from you to him? Is that how little you think of me?'

His face had darkened. 'Didn't you think that of me?'

'And didn't I have cause to?'

A look of desperation crossed his face. 'Look, Poppy, before you go I'd like to explain something to you—but we can't have a slanging match here in the corridor. Won't you come into the office, just for a moment?'

She knew she shouldn't—what was the point? Yet she wanted to hear what he had to say. 'All right,' she said. 'But just for a moment.'

Fergus held the door open for her formally and gestured towards a chair. 'Would you like to sit down?'

'I'd prefer to stand, thank you.'

'Well, I'm tired of standing—I've been on my feet all day.' He perched on the edge of the table, and as she saw the lines of weariness etched deep into the craggy face, Poppy knew a pang of sympathy. She was reminded of the first time she had met him, when he had perched in the same place, and had picked up a textbook and begun to read, forgetting she was there. He had grown thinner too, she thought critically, and his face looked as if it hadn't seen any fresh air lately.

'I don't know how to say all this,' he said wearily.

'But whatever you may think, I just want you to know that I wasn't seeing Catherine as well as you.'

'But I heard you speak to her on the telephone—you took the call downstairs, and when I came down I heard you arranging to meet her. And you couldn't tell me it was all over between you, could you?' Her voice had begun to shake as she relived the awful scene.

Fergus sighed. 'I can explain, but won't you please sit down? It's hurting my neck to look up at you.'

'Oh, all right,' she said ungraciously. She sat down on the desk too, taking great care to sit as far away from him as possible.

He frowned with the effort of trying to explain. 'I'd been going out with Catherine for a long time—almost eight years. We met as registrars and hit it off immediately. By that time we were both bored with the constant changing of partners—I was looking for a more stabilising influence in my life, and so was she.'

'Go on,' said Poppy, furious with herself for the wild flash of jealousy that swept through her at his words.

'But at the end of our registrarships—we moved to different hospitals—it was always understood that our careers took precedence over everything else. We continued to see one another when work allowed, which wasn't usually more than once or twice a month.' Fergus picked up a pencil and began to turn it round and round between his fingers.

'We'd been drifting apart for ages, so gradually that we hardly noticed it. Or at least I didn't, but then I was too busy. . .' He stopped for a moment. 'Oh, what the hell!' he exclaimed. 'Why shouldn't you know? I was too busy falling in love with you to notice anything.'

He couldn't really be saying this, Poppy reasoned, and took a deep breath to calm herself.

'And so was Catherine—falling in love, that is.' He turned to face her, seeing that he now had her total attention. 'She began seeing Philip over six months ago. Do you remember—she brought him to my Christmas party? She couldn't understand why I didn't say something then, why I chose to ignore it—but that night all I could think about was you, Poppy.

'All I'm trying to tell you is that I haven't been seeing Catherine, that our relationship has been non-existent, in all the time I've known you. There's been no deception or betrayal, either to you or to her. That's all.'

That's all, he had said. As if that wasn't enough, Poppy thought, her heart giving a great leap of happiness, but he hadn't finished.

'Catherine rang that morning to arrange to meet me, because she wanted to tell me that she and Philip are getting married. She said that what we'd shared had been friendship and habit more than anything else, and that she'd fallen in love at last. And when we did meet she told me it was as plain as day that I was madly in love with you, and that I should get in touch with you and tell you.'

'Then why didn't you?' cried Poppy.

Fergus shook his head. 'I felt bad about the loose

ends I'd left untied, about the fact that you thought I'd deceived you. I tried to write so many times, but the right words wouldn't come.

'Then I saw you each day at James's bedside and, I convinced myself that it was him you really wanted, that it was him you loved, that he was closer in age to you, more fun. . . The whole hospital was talking about it. I thought I'd simply read far too much into what was never intended to be more than a very wonderful evening. . .'

'Oh, Fergus, you've got it all wrong. James has never been more than a very dear friend to me. I was as much to blame for what happened as you. I assumed that Catherine was off the scene—there'd been no contact between you in all the time I'd been staying with you, so I pushed any questions about her to the back of my mind, because I wanted what was about to happen so much. And so when she rang that morning I thought the worst—I felt so rotten inside and I took it all out on you—leaping to the wrong conclusions. I said some terrible things to you. . .'

'I wasn't particularly pleasant to you either,' Fergus said softly.

'I deserved it.'

'No, you didn't—I shouldn't have procrastinated.'

'Oh, Fergus!'

He was staring at her. 'You mean—you don't hate me?'

Poppy actually laughed aloud. 'Hate you? Are you mad, Fergus Browne? I love you. I've loved you for months—surely you knew that?'

He stared at her, the expression on his face that of someone who had found a treasure they'd been searching for for a very long time. He shook his head in disbelief. 'I thought you just told me that you loved me,' he said.

'Not loved,' she corrected. 'Love—present tense. I love you, Fergus.'

'Poppy, darling!' He gave a kind of yelp and jumped to his feet, pulling her into his arms, those strong arms she had never thought to feel again. 'Will you say it once more, in case I'm dreaming?'

'I love you. I love you. I love you. How's that?' she smiled.

He sighed against her mouth. 'You darling, beautiful girl! I love you too. I was lying beside you that morning, so—so—oh, I don't know—overjoyed with the mystery of it all and longing to tell you. In love, properly in love, for the first time in my life, and then everything started to go wrong. I thought I'd blown it.'

She turned her large violet eyes to his. 'Can you ever forgive me for the things I accused you of?'

'It's forgotten,' he murmured, then halted all further conversation by kissing her.

'Fergus,' she said at last, 'do you think it will matter about us—I mean, won't everyone talk? You're so senior, and I'm just. . .'

'Hush!' he said fiercely. 'Don't ever say that again. You're everything to me, Poppy. You've put me in touch with a part of myself I never knew existed— I'd only ever scratched the surface before. I love you so much,' he whispered, and she felt the tears prick at her eyes. He bent his head to hers, but she stopped him with a mischievous look on her face.

'Do you remember the first time you kissed me?'

'Of course I do!' he said, as proudly as if he had just invented a cure for the common cold. 'It was just before Christmas at my party, and very conventional—beneath the mistletoe.'

'It wasn't, you know!'

He frowned. 'Some amnesiac episode in my past?'

'Exactly!' Poppy exclaimed delightedly. 'When I looked after you when you were ill, I was in the process of dosing you up with some pills and you pulled me on to the bed and started to kiss me.'

'Did I, now?' Fergus murmured.

'Yes, you did!'

'And how did I kiss you, tell me? Like this?' He kissed her softly.

'Er—not exactly.'

'Like this, then?'

'You're getting warmer!'

'Surely not like. . .this. . .'

'Mmm, *just* like that!' she whispered.

His eyes twinkled. 'You must have thought me a terrible man, Miss Henderson?'

She laughed, with all the confidence of a woman who knows she is loved. 'I rather enjoyed it, actually,' she told him.

'Come here!'

Their breath had begun to quicken. 'Let's go home to bed,' Fergus said simply. 'If I carry on kissing you here, I might just be tempted to lock the door and make love to you on my examining couch!'

'Fergus!' She blushed.

He gave her the enchanting grin which had first captivated her. 'And, even though I *am* head of department, it would hardly do for a senior consult-ant to be found making love to his wife-to-be on hospital premises!'

'Wife-to-be?' Poppy squeaked.

He looked down at her anxiously. 'That is, if you'll have me? I've spent all these years finding you—I don't want to lose you now. You will marry me, won't you, Poppy?'

She smiled as she wrapped her arms around his neck. 'Fergus, love,' she whispered tenderly, 'some-times, for an intelligent man, you can be a real eejit!'

MARCH 1991 HARDBACK TITLES

— ROMANCE —

Leave Love Alone *Lindsay Armstrong*	3460	0 263 12735 4
A Cinderella Affair *Anne Beaumont*	3461	0 263 12736 2
When the Devil Drives *Sara Craven*	3462	0 263 12737 0
The Iron Master *Rachel Ford*	3463	0 263 12738 9
A Special Sort of Man *Natalie Fox*	3464	0 263 12739 7
Breaking the Ice *Kay Gregory*	3465	0 263 12740 0
Steps to Heaven *Sally Heywood*	3466	0 263 12741 9
Payment Due *Penny Jordan*	3467	0 263 12742 7
Mistaken Love *Shirley Kemp*	3468	0 263 12743 5
Master of Marshlands *Miriam Macgregor*	3469	0 263 12744 3
Land of Dragons *Joanna Mansell*	3470	0 263 12745 1
A Fiery Encounter *Margaret Mayo*	3471	0 263 12746 X
Flight of Discovery *Jessica Steele*	3472	0 263 12747 8
The Devil's Kiss *Sally Wentworth*	3473	0 263 12748 6
Valley of the Devil *Yvonne Whittal*	3474	0 263 12749 4
Broken Dreams *Jennifer Williams*	3475	0 263 12750 8

MASQUERADE *Historical*

A Woman of Little Importance *Sheila Walsh*	M259	0 263 12771 0
The Black Pearl *Laura Cassidy*	M260	0 263 12772 9

MEDICAL ROMANCE

Give Me Tomorrow *Sarah Franklin*	D177	0 263 12777 X
Specialist in Love *Sharon Wirdnam*	D178	0 263 12778 8

LARGE PRINT

Bride of Diamonds *Emma Darcy*	407	0 263 12561 0
A Civilised Arrangement *Catherine George*	408	0 263 12562 9
An Insatiable Passion *Lynne Graham*	409	0 263 12563 7
Game of Love *Penny Jordan*	410	0 263 12564 5
An Impossible Situation *Margaret Mayo*	411	0 263 12565 3
A Casual Affair *Susanne McCarthy*	412	0 263 12566 1
An Accidental Affair *Elizabeth Oldfield*	413	0 263 12567 X
Curtain of Stars *Patricia Wilson*	414	0 263 12568 8

Mills & Boon

APRIL 1991 HARDBACK TITLES

─── ROMANCE ───

Passionate Betrayal *Jacqueline Baird*	3476	0 263 12751 6
A Promise to Repay *Amanda Browning*	3477	0 263 12752 4
Happy Ending *Sandra Field*	3478	0 263 12753 2
An Unequal Partnership *Rosemary Gibson*	3479	0 263 12754 0
Angela's Affair *Vanessa Grant*	3480	0 263 12755 9
Windswept *Rosalie Henaghan*	3481	0 263 12756 7
Kiss and Say Goodbye *Stephanie Howard*	3482	0 263 12757 5
Shotgun Wedding *Charlotte Lamb*	3483	0 263 12758 3
Scandalous Seduction *Miranda Lee*	3484	0 263 12759 1
Tiger Moon *Kristy McCallum*	3485	0 263 12760 5
That Long-ago Summer *Sandra Marton*	3486	0 263 12761 3
Such Sweet Poison *Anne Mather*	3487	0 263 12762 1
Backlash *Elizabeth Oldfield*	3488	0 263 12763 X
The Price of Desire *Kate Proctor*	3489	0 263 12764 8
Perilous Refuge *Patricia Wilson*	3490	0 263 12765 6
Fully Involved *Rebecca Winters*	3491	0 263 12766 4

MASQUERADE *Historical*

Brighton Masquerade *Petra Nash*	M261	0 263 12862 8
Rebel by Moonlight *Elaine Reeve*	M262	0 263 12863 6

MEDICAL ROMANCE

Goodbye to Yesterday *Sarah Franklin*	D179	0 263 12868 7
Calling Nurse Hillier *Elizabeth Petty*	D180	0 263 12869 5

LARGE PRINT

A Summer Storm *Robyn Donald*	415	0 263 12593 9
Time to Let Go *Alison Fraser*	416	0 263 12594 7
The Wrong Kind of Man *Rosemary Hammond*	417	0 263 12595 5
A Kind of Madness *Penny Jordan*	418	0 263 12596 3
Lightning Strike *Marjorie Lewty*	419	0 263 12597 1
A Suitable Match *Betty Neels*	420	0 263 12598 X
Lovespell *Jennifer Taylor*	421	0 263 12599 8
Sicilian Vengeance *Sara Wood*	422	0 263 12600 5